SYLVIA PLATH WATCHES US SLEEP ...BUT WE DON'T MIND

Victoria Richards

First published June 2023 by Fly on the Wall Press
Published in the UK by
Fly on the Wall Press
The Wentwood
72-76 Newton St
Manchester
M1 1EW
www.flyonthewallpress.co.uk
ISBN: 9781913211899
Copyright Victoria Richards © 2023

A CIP Catalogue record for this book is available from the British Library.

For my friends, who keep me steady.
You are beloved.

CONTENTS

NEVER RUN FROM WILD DOGS

I give a handful of change to Naomi, the deaf girl who sits outside the entrance, sleeping bag bunched wet around her waist like a ball gown. Cross the road. Pass a gaggle of boys taking turns to punch each other in the leg and shout 'faggot'; marvel that it's still an insult, after all this time, even for Gen Alpha. Glance back, over my shoulder, towards the lights. The 101 is unpredictable these days. Yesterday, a seventeen-minute wait. This morning, nineteen. There's nothing on the horizon except the girl at the bus stop.

It is raining. I should've noticed — Naomi's sodden sleeping bag, the water running sideways as I came out of the hot space underground, mounted the escalators, passed posters for *The Lion King* and a poem that doesn't rhyme, doesn't even scan properly, though perhaps it doesn't matter so long as it reminds you to get off the train if you feel sick or to make room for others or to *see it, say it, sorted*. Night-shifters making their way down the jagged steps on the other side, shaking off umbrellas, fat and swollen. Their downturned mouths. If I'd been more observant I would've sworn and said, "I should've worn my coat", though it doesn't fit, not now, not over my round belly. And so it goes.

I draw close to the girl in the red shelter. Close enough to take in all the details I can, all the details she puts out on offer. Short black hair, dissecting the softness of her chin. Fringe cut clean across her forehead. Face so symmetrical I can hardly bear it. Teeth white and strong, blunt at the edges, like horse teeth, a sliver of a gap between the front

7

two. Eyes wide and clear and lichen green. Her hair is wet and she is crying. I want to tell her what I remember from that TV programme about facing down wild dogs. *If you are overwhelmed and unable to stay on your feet, do what your instincts should be telling you to do: duck and cover.*

Her white school shirt is short-sleeved, despite the weather. It is sodden and so, translucent. She has a schoolgirl tattoo on her right forearm – a blue biro penis – and on her left I can just make out the faded word *LOVE*, in capitals. Love is always in capitals.

She holds her burgundy blazer out between two fingers like it might bite her. "Is it wet?" I'll say in five minutes or so, once I've plucked up courage, and she'll nod pointlessly, and I'll reach out to stroke the worn lining inside it instead of hugging her like I want to and nod back. She is shivering. The crowd sways and undulates. The audience is uneasy.

"It's a bad situation to be in," a girl of about her age says, which is fourteen, or fifteen, half mine.

"Well bad," a boy agrees. "But she can't do anything about it."

They are talking about her like she doesn't exist, and I wonder if the girl wants it that way, if that is entirely the point. She looks out away from them across the green, one solitary tear carving a path through the concrete of her cheek. She has no distinct expression. She doesn't look pissed off that water runs clear into those algae eyes, or that her hair is plastered to her forehead. It doesn't seem to bother her that her teeth are cymbals, her nostrils marionettes. She doesn't notice the brass band that plays across her face (that beautiful face).

I back into the shelter. The kids behind me take up all the space. I am pissed off because I am old. I am entitled. I am – *almost* – mother. My laptop is getting wet in the yellow rucksack on my back and *do they know how expensive it is? More than their pocket money for an entire year... five years!* Water drips off the broken spoke of my umbrella and hits someone's shoes. I don't say sorry.

"I'm scared," the girl says suddenly, as though she's been prompted. Her voice breaks in the middle.

"Take this," a boy offers. He is a year or two older than her. He's been listening – watching – and sees himself as the hero, you can tell. With his long, dark lashes, his nicotine eyes. He wears a black leather jacket. It clashes with the uncertainty he keeps in his front pocket.

She doesn't look at him. Keeps her eyes trained on empty. "No, thanks."

"Take it," he insists. "It's zone six. It'll get you all the way to the airport."

The airport? The stakes have risen. We've entered a whole new level with the mention of planes and tarmac and the promise of escape. It's deeper than the set-up: it's like a killer with a distinctive scar, a left-handed thief. There's more to this story now we've got an airport. The question is: where is she going, and why?

"She doesn't want it," her friend says, looking at her sideways. The girl backs her up with a short shake of her head. *Phew*, the friend must be thinking. *I got that right.*

"Take it," our hero tries again. He's persistent. That's what they wrote on the casting call: *Young, dark, handsome. Calm, even in the middle of a shipwreck or storm. Wears leather jacket, is ultimately undermined by desperation.* You can see how much he wants to be the one to fix this. Soon enough, he begins to lose patience, his machismo turning soggy around the edges. "Just give it to her," he snaps.

He thrusts the flimsy travel card at the friend, but she's just a bit-part. She has no more lines to say. She receives it and clutches it to her chest where it gleams pinkly, like salmon.

"I'm so fucking scared," the girl says suddenly. Her voice is low and halting. It scratches my skin and I forget myself. Turn 90 degrees to look directly at her, which hurts. I need sunglasses.

"What are you scared of?" I ask her.

The crowd starts to murmur. This is not the way it was supposed to go. This is a one-act play. Nobody's rehearsed for an interval. They feel duped. In a moment they'll be angry. I talk quickly before the blood-lust comes. When it does, there'll be no point in running. *Running is exactly what they want you to do, that's how they hunt. They run their prey tired and then finish them off after they can't run any further.*

She shrugs. Mumbles. "My mum."

I understand. I remember the way mine used to snap and growl and bite and tear, the way she'd bristle, hackles high and sharp as mountains. I remember the sharpness of her teeth, her forked tongue. I remember being scared.

"I've got to do my homework," I'd tell her, like it made any difference. "I've got an exam." I'd back away slowly, calmly, roll my hands into fists to protect my fingers. *Don't make direct eye contact. Don't smile. Don't make any sudden moves. Try talking calmly. Above all, don't act like food.*

Still, I couldn't stop myself shaking like something

weak and half-cooked as she tore the kitchen apart, smashed the plate I made her when I was six, purple hand-prints splashed bright in the centre. Grandma's pie dish split in two. Ninety-six silver shards of Uncle Len's whiskey glass gathered themselves together like a malformed butterfly and struggled towards the window. Memories pooled, blood red, across the dirty lino. *Trying to run away will show weakness and trigger their prey drive. Your job is to act bored until they aren't interested in you, then to slowly back away.*

"Go to the shop," she'd say, throwing me a fiver. "Get me something to drink."

"I can't buy what you want with a fiver," I didn't say. What she wanted was the hard stuff — fire in a glass, liquid anaesthesia. Mr Singh at *Singh's Premier Store* had plastic bottles of cider, £2.99. Cheap, fizzy, tasted of apples. Mr Singh sighed as he gave me the change. "Tell your mum she owes me rent," he said. I told her and the telling took three weeks to fade.

I want to tell the girl it gets better — that it will all be okay — but I don't. Can't. "Is it wet?" I say instead, nodding at her blazer like I knew I would. I reach out and stroke its soft insides. It is damp mud and rotting leaves. It is silkworms weaving and spinning and slow, circular dancing.

"I've lost my bus pass," the girl says, like I've asked a different question. Perhaps I have. "I've got to get to the airport."

"What time?"

"Eight."

"What are you doing until eight?"

"Rain."

Rain. What an answer. What a bold, epic answer. Rain as verb, rain as doing. Rain as everything unsaid. It lifts me up. I want to break into thunderous applause, demand an encore. But the crowd has gone and we are alone and I can't stop talking.

"You know," I say. "It is *just* a bus pass. I'm sure your mum won't mind."

Just. Such simple, four-lettered devastation. It was *just* one drink, always *just* one. It was *just* one as she lay face-down in a puddle of her own vomit, *just* one as blue lights bounced against our windows in the dark street, the neighbours peering like ghosts. *Just* one in the hospital bed, hooked up to cord and wire and slow *beep-beep-beeping*, a broken egg yolk in a sea of starched white. And, after, *just* one more. The last one more.

"Sorry," I say, and the girl blinks. "That was a stupid thing to say." Pause. Ten seconds. Twenty. Thirty. Then — "What will you do?"

She looks up. Is she looking for an answer? To see if the rain has stopped? Is she looking for God in the empty sky?

"I don't know."

Something over my shoulder catches her attention. She looks past me at a crimson wave breaking over the horizon. The W19.

"It's my bus," she says, moving away from the shelter. Her voice rises an octave. There is hope in it, or perhaps it is catharsis.

"You'll be okay," I say, pushing my umbrella towards her. She slaps it away but I stand firm. I am insistent. I am protector. We battle silently over cheap black nylon.

"Thank you," she says, as I move out into the wet to watch her get on.

It's not your fault, I want to say. That's what the priest said to me at Mum's funeral, though I didn't believe him. It felt fitting, somehow, to put her in a box. She always said she wanted to move away from our nasty flat with its bad dreams and soggy ceilings and disappointment. I chose the cheapest coffin going – cardboard with white rope handles. Got the eulogy from a free sample on a website called *Loving Loss.com*.

"My mother was a person you could really depend on," I read out blankly. "She was a rock." Scattered applause from the handful of mourners. I'd get no five-star reviews. And while I was talking, I kept getting distracted. Kept thinking of those feral dogs.

On the ground, pull your knees tight to your chest. Tuck your head down, chin to chest. Stay quiet. Don't move or scream. You are hoping the dogs will quickly lose interest, and/or that help will arrive before it's too late. This move is called 'last resort'.

SYLVIA PLATH WATCHES US SLEEP,
BUT WE DON'T MIND

We've been married three years when Sylvia Plath appears in our bedroom. There is a chair in the corner, an old French Louis XV-style copy in walnut and cream. The seat is soft, flecked with grey fur at the edges where the cat likes to sit. The cat doesn't sit there anymore, though. There's no space. Where there was once the cat, now sits Sylvia.

When I first see her there, collar like a ruff of white lace around her neck, I assume she is a new cleaner sent by the agency, that she is waiting for me to give her instructions on bleach versus white vinegar, to tell her whether we want our sheets ironed or left creased, because of the bedspread. (Nobody can see what's beneath the covers if there's a bedspread.) You can leave behind the detritus of a day— toast, those crunchy, black paper envelopes that hold After Eights, condoms, tear-splatter stripes of mascara. Life's hidden intimacies.

She sits on the chair *just so*, and I realise she can't be a cleaner. She crosses her legs at the ankle, like she doesn't have anywhere else to be. Doesn't say anything. Just looks at me, her face open yet closed at the same time. It is a look that says, *I see you*. I stare back at her, confused, and then it dawns on me that it is eleven at night and you are downstairs, watching TV, and it is Friday, and she is Sylvia Plath.

I know her from the reddish-brown of her hair, the girlish Alice band, the plainness of her dress, her eyes. Those haunted eyes. I know her from that old copy of *The Colossus* from 1998, a first edition, the one we have on the bookshelf with her name in orange on the front. *The Colossus and Other Poems*. She sits on the cover like she is sitting on our chair: young, cross-legged and decidedly, stubbornly alive. Yet I know she is dead. I know that she took her own life at 30, the age I am now. I know this. Questions hang in the air like smoke.

Ten… nine… eight… I let most of my breath out in one go, like the helium in that shiny-red, heart-shaped balloon you gave me with some flowers for my birthday. I moved it from room to room, hoping it would snag on a nail, the cat would prick it with a razor claw, hoping it would wither. In the end, I snipped it with scissors in the kitchen when you weren't looking and stuffed it in the bin.

Three… two…. My lungs deflate, making me dizzy. I breathe in again, look at Sylvia and nod. She nods back. We share a mutual sense of resignation. Then she settles back against the chair, her hands neatly stacked in her lap.

Your shoes are heavy on the stairs. They make the glass lights on the ceiling below jingle and shake. You come into the bedroom. You look from me to Sylvia and back again. Spit foams at the corners of your mouth. You remind me of a goldfish with pop-eye.

"What the fuck is *she* doing here?" You point accusingly, as though she is mine.

I shrug. "I don't know," I say. This makes you madder.

"What do you mean you *don't know*?" Your voice has risen a couple of octaves. It sounds the way you sounded when we were fourteen, when you'd throw gravel at the porch to let me know you were waiting, leaving a spider-web of cracked glass. I'd tell Dad I was going for milk and slip out of the door sideways, in a dress with lemons embroidered on the collar. I would mutter, "Alright?", my heart a snare, and climb up on the saddle behind you. I'd press my face into the back of your black-and-white striped Adidas tracksuit top and close my eyes, breathing in ash and beer and salt. My toes would drag along the concrete as we coasted down the hill and it would burn red-hot but I wouldn't lift my feet up.

"How did she get in? Did you let her in?" I stare at him, my lips sealed tight like clams. "Why isn't she talking? Jesus Christ, what the fuck is *wrong* with her? Is she homeless or something?" You go close to Sylvia, wave your hand in front of her face, punch the wall. Paint scatters.

It goes on like this. You're still talking, but I can't make out the words, and I wonder if I've gone deaf, or if your voice is so high with rage that it's reached that mosquito alarm pitch only young people can hear. We're not young anymore, so I can't hear you.We're not young anymore.Later, after you've stalked off to the bathroom to brush your teeth, to shave, you get into bed, one eye on the chair, watchful and wary. You are wearing the underpants I asked you to throw away two Christmases ago, the ones that hang down to your knees.

"Is she just going to sit there like that, or what?" you say, grunting with displeasure the way you grunt when someone asks us for money when we're outside a restaurant.

I shrug again, but this time I don't say I don't know. We sleep.

You've left for work by the time I wake up, and I don't know if you kissed me goodbye. I feel sluggish and press myself deeper into my pillow, tiredness like a coat I can't take off. Then I remember her. *Sylvia.* I open my eyes and rub grit from the corners. I stare at the ceiling. I imagine what I'll say when you come home, when I tell you about the dream I had.

"I dreamed Sylvia Plath was sitting on that chair in the corner of our bedroom," I'll say, my voice sounding both amused and tinged with irony. "We had a fight about it. You punched a wall." I'll probably run my fingers through my hair in that way you once said made me look cute. I'll be ready to laugh or to dismiss the conversation, depending on how your day has gone. You'll say, "Who?", as disinterested as if she was someone I work with.

I push myself up on my elbows, shaking off pins and needles. I look across the room to the chair, and there she is.

She's wearing different clothes today. A cardigan, heavy wool, though the heating is on and the brass thermometer on the bedroom wall reads 22 degrees. There is a brown-and-white checked hem running from her neck to her waist, decorated with buttons. She is pregnant, which is strange, because in that instant I realise that I am too.

"*Of course,*" I think, staring with wonder at Sylvia Plath, at her belly's gentle roundness, at her sober smile. She wears the same downturned lips and high cheekbones as yesterday. I guess she is six months – *seven?* – gone. I know it the way pensioners in the street tell young women who didn't ask that it's 'definitely a boy'.

I feel it stir somewhere deep within me; tiny, sunflower seed, not 2mm long. I picture myself like Sylvia, months from now, belly like a road map, filled with the whirls and ripples of impatient life. I imagine myself, stumbling from bed, cow-heavy and floral, like her *Morning Song*.

I wonder what you'll say when I tell you. The last time, the time it didn't work, you grew flat and distant. I used to catch you staring into space, your hand close to your mouth but not quite touching. If I asked, you'd look at me blankly for a few seconds, then say, "Huh?" and, "I'm fine", but the top of your nose would wrinkle with irritation. I couldn't help myself. I asked you ten, twenty times a day, willing you to give me any other answer but 'fine', willing myself to believe you.

"This time," I say to Sylvia, determined, nodding my head like it makes a difference, "it'll be okay. This time it'll stick."

I place the flat of my hand against the softness of my belly. This time, I tell her, I will do pregnancy yoga and antenatal classes. I won't skip out because I am embarrassed by the demonstrations, by the teacher's giant, woolly model of a vagina, by the photos of huge, swollen women who don't look a bit like me in birth pools, stained red. I'll take 400 micrograms of folic acid every day, and extra iron, and omega-3s. I'll stop smoking. Drinking. Coffee, vodka. Maybe even wine. I won't clean out the cat's litter tray when it's overflowing and stinking, that will be your job, and I'll stop eating cheese with mould in it. I'll go to bed early and I'll — we'll — take a photo of my belly, every week. We'll go for gentle walks in the forest on Sundays and I'll set aside two, five to ten-minute periods of the day, every day, for mindfulness, to bond with the baby. I'll even join an NCT group.

"Did you do all of those things?" I ask Sylvia, doubtfully. She places her left hand on her belly – she looks about eight months pregnant, I decide, not six – and stares dolefully out of the window.

"I was amazed when I found how easy she was," she tells me but doesn't tell me: Ted and Sylvia, 1961, an interview, uploaded to YouTube. I place the words in Sylvia's mouth now, like a kiss. "I had wondered if I would feel swallowed up by motherhood and never have any time to myself. But somehow, she fitted in beautifully."

"You loved Ted, didn't you?" I ask. I fancy she is telling me with her eyes what I've read about, about how she wanted to meet Ted Hughes because she'd read some of his poems, and she'd been impressed by him, and they went to a party in London, and then somehow, ended up married.

I think about how we ended up married. It didn't begin at a party, like Sylvia and Ted, but at the back of the bus, in 2001. You called me 'babe' and stuck your hand down my top to feel the silky lining of my bra.

We 'did it' for the first time two weeks later in the park in Bethnal Green, after it was dark and the wardens had locked the gates. You helped me climb over the metal spikes. I put my hand in somebody else's piss and wiped it on my jeans, but you didn't mind. You held it anyway and led me to a bench where we drank cheap, warm cider that tasted like sweets. It made my head spin as I looked up at the stars. *This*, I thought. *This is the love I dreamed of.*

'It' happened. I could feel the wet grass against my back, the cold air on my thighs. It was rough, like holding my hand under the cold tap until it was numb and aching;

hot, like carpet burn on my knees; sharp, like the stitches the doctor said I had to have, and I knew I had to have them, though every fibre in my body wanted to pull away. When it was over, you kissed me and said I was special, that you'd never let me go.

I lay back against the pillows again and ask Sylvia what it was like for her as a child. "I was happy, up to the age of about nine, very carefree and I believed in magic," she says-said through the small speaker in my phone. "At nine I was rather disillusioned. I stopped believing in elves and Santa Claus and became more realistic and depressed."

I nod sympathetically. "I understand," I say.

When I was a child, everything was cold and I had to sit in my room while my parents got drunk in the kitchen. I would stay perfectly still in the quiet dark, listening to them laugh and joke and fizz and sometimes my mother would stamp upstairs and throw open the door and hiss, her teeth bared like the wild cats in the alley next to the supermarket. Sometimes she'd grab my arm so tight it would leave bruises and tell me I was a 'bad girl'.

I like it when *you* call me a "bad girl", though. I know it turns you on, because you growl a little bit and slap me and say, "*oh, yeah, oh, fuck, yeah.*"

I tell Sylvia about the day my mother died. I was nine, and she forgot to pick me up from school, and so I walked home, and climbed through a window because I didn't have a key. Inside, everything was messy and smelled of wet, and she was in the kitchen, slumped over a bowl of milk. The milk had a film across the top of it, like custard. I touched her and she was a mannequin, one of those plastic women with both

21

arms cut blunt at the wrist, smile fixed, eyes blue and glazed. She wasn't my mother anymore. I wondered if she ever was.

Thinking about this makes me feel sad. I get up and put on a dress, something pink to draw my mind towards daylight. I go downstairs and watch TV, and somehow, the day passes. Nervous moths bash and crash into my ribcage.

When you come home, you don't hug me or say hello. You slump on the sofa in your crumpled suit, the remote-control slack in your hand, your laces undone and trailing like worms on the carpet.

"I've got something to tell you," I swallow, hovering at the edges. You sigh and nod your head sideways to tell me I'm in the way of the TV.

"I'm pregnant," I say, biting my lip until I taste blood.

You turn to me, frowning. "What?"

"Pregnant," I repeat.

You stare at me. The remote slips from your hand and clatters off the sofa to the floor. You press your fingers to your temples. You breathe in, your cheeks filled with air, and out, in one, quick burst. You push yourself up with your hands and stand. The sudden movement makes me flinch. I take a step back.

"I'm going for a walk," you say, not looking at me as you leave the room. I put my arms around myself and hug myself tight as the front door slams. I don't know when you'll be back. The cat wanders in and winds himself around my legs like a question.

Above my head, the glass lights jingle and shake like bells, and I feel an aching. I stare up at the ceiling and wonder

if Sylvia has gone or if she'll stay another night, tonight —
please, just one more night — and watch over us while we sleep.

DROWNING DOESN'T LOOK LIKE DROWNING

Except in rare circumstances, drowning people are physiologically unable to call out for help. The respiratory system was designed for breathing. Speech is the secondary or overlaid function. Breathing must be fulfilled before speech occurs.

He turns grey, head bobbing in the angry spray. Stares straight ahead at some invisible angel, grim and determined, while his mouth opens and closes in a silent staccato. Maybe this is what they mean when they say you meet your maker. You have to look hard, search deep inside yourself, when the time comes. Face fate with your hands down. Nobody tells you how quiet it is, though. Death like an old coin, dropping into the deep.

*

The sun throbs over Havana. It dusts the shoulders of tourists, tanned and swollen, groups of kids barefoot at the corners of the big hotels. Security guards shoo them away but they keep coming back, like pups with brand new tricks.

"Hey, lady! You like Cuban music? Come, I take you to hear real music!"

"Miss! Do you know the capital of France? Paris. One dollar, any capital. Try me!"

I slip on to the road past beige pensioners being pushed to the pavement by tiny hustlers. A small boy grins at me sideways as he yanks the sole of a large American away from the dust and into his lap. He reaches into his pocket and whips out a tool kit: screwdriver, four shiny nails, a small block heel he measures against the pillowy underside of the man's size 10 Nike Air. He holds firm and begins to tap.

A spool of little girls attach themselves to me as I drift through the Malecón, with its run-down yellows and pinks, jazz beating from open doorways. They giggle at my elbow, clothes torn, hair black and unravelled. Eyes bright as peonies. Small hands reach up to my shoulders to tug-tug-tug at my t-shirt. Their mouths make circles as they trail silvery-blonde between dirty fingers.

"Muy bonita," they say.

"Yo no!" I shake my head, point at them softly. "*Ustedes* son muy bonitas."

I pull away to squeeze down a side-alley, where wrought iron black gates mark the courtyard entrance in the grounds of a small hotel. There is a round table in the middle, set up for breakfast. Domed gauze covers plates of pastries, cured meats, envelopes of cheese with holes punched in the middle. Flies buzz around but can't find a way in, settling reproachfully on a stack of white plates. I smile at the waiter who greeted me yesterday.

"Buenos días."

"Buenos días, señorita."

He gestures to the table to tell me to help myself. He doesn't seem to mind me being there, though it's clear I'm no guest. There are only a handful of rooms in this boutique place. They probably know everyone by sight already, maybe even by name. The place is bright and fresh, a stark contrast to our cramped apartment just a couple of streets away. I hate the cheap Airbnb already and we've only been here three days. It has a dodgy lift that looks exactly the same as in that Spanish horror film we watched back at home, the one where something unspeakable happens but the lights are out and the only way to see it is through a camera with night vision. My husband rolled his eyes when I said I was scared and kept up a horrible, low-pitched growling noise in the darkness of our bed, then laughed when it made me cry. I wave my hands in the sunlight to focus on something else and take a piece of bread. I don't want to think about London, not here in this shimmering place.

"Dónde está tu novio?" The waiter flashes his teeth. They are strong and white. The corners of his lips curve upwards like he's asking something different.

"No tengo novio." I shake my head. "Tengo un marido." I hold up my left hand. The gold band catches the light. "Estamos de luna de miel." I looked up how to say it before we came away. I thought it romantic – honeymoon, *luna de miel*. Moon made of honey.

"De qué está corriendo, señora?"

The waiter lays out knives on starched white cotton, like he's preparing bodies for burial. I make a pumping motion with my arms, not sure I've understood.

"Corriendo?"

He nods. A smile breaks over his lips. I wish he'd go back to calling me señorita.

27

"I'm not running," I say slowly. He raises his eyebrows but doesn't reply. I turn away from the table and sit on a small white bench, nibbling breadcrumbs like popcorn. It is chewy, slightly salty. Could be fresher. It was probably made yesterday, not at four this morning, not like at Fabien's, the sweet old guy who runs the French bakery on Hackney Road.

Every weekend I wake at six and slip out of the sheets like butter, pull on my running gear in the velvet dark. Outside, the skin on my arms is rough and stippled. I suck London down in lungfuls as I pound the road: fryer grease, spatters of vomit. Dog shit and vodka and the tangy ripeness of bin bags torn open by foxes. I could draw a map of the city based on its smells. Each scent a landmark, or life buoy. I would start and end at Fabien's, with oven-warm baguettes and eclairs and coffee and cream and the feeling of belonging.

Fabien and I have a careful routine. He tuts about having to get up while it's still dark, talks about his wife and daughters with a kind of reverence. I listen quietly, lick almond paste from my fingers. It is our communion.

I pat my pocket for my phone, think irrationally of ringing in, of ringing England to tell Fabien why I hadn't appeared like usual on Saturday. He would've made me an espresso. I can picture it growing cold on top of the counter, paper cup sagging wet and soft. I hadn't even told him about the wedding.

Drowning people's mouths alternately sink below and reappear above the surface of the water. The mouths of drowning people are not above the surface of the water long enough for them to exhale, inhale, or call out for help.

The waiter stands in front of me and shifts from foot to foot like he wants to say something. He gazes at the sky as if it holds the answer, or at least, a handy Spanish-to-English dictionary. Opens his mouth. His tongue is wide and pink and wet and for a moment I imagine it buried between my legs, twisting and searching and dragging *te quiero* out of me.

"You like fishes?"

He moves his hand up and down, undulating his fingers like they are a shoal and the air a slip-stream.

"Sí."

He nods, looks relieved. Holds one finger up then disappears through white slatted doors. I wait, listening to the clatter and rattle of pans being washed in the kitchen, a radio playing a fast Latin beat, tuneful whistling. Someone somewhere is cooking *ropa vieja*: shredded steak, peppers, onions. The smell of it makes my stomach hurt.

The waiter comes back with a scrap of paper and hands it to me. I read the numbers like they'll tell me what to do, not just here but away from here. Not just now, but always.

"Luis. My friend." He makes the sign of a phone next to his ear and chin. "Take you to see fishes. Beautiful coral in Cuba. The best." He kisses his fingers.

"Gracias."

Drowning people cannot wave for help. Nature instinctively forces them to extend their arms laterally and press down on the water's surface. Pressing down on the surface of the water permits drowning people to use their bodies as leverage so they can lift their mouths out of the water to breathe.

When I get back to the apartment, my husband is still in bed, squinting at his phone.

"I went for a run," I lie. I pull the elastic from my hair and shake it out, massage my scalp. I think of the little girls and their small hands, skin brown and smooth as chestnuts. I wonder how long it will be before their sweetness fades, before the soles of their feet turn hard and black from walking barefoot over gravel. Before their fingers learn tricks their minds turn away from. I wonder if they'll hide their regrets like I did, with drink and a razor's sweet relief.

"Maybe we can go snorkelling tomorrow? I got the number of a guy who can take us." I throw the words back over my shoulder as I pull off my shorts. Nothing. I turn to check he's listening, t-shirt damp against my chest. He scowls and reaches out of bed to pull the curtains shut to see the screen better.

"Did you hear me?"

"What?" He glances up but it doesn't quite reach me. "Yeah."

I close the door to the small en-suite, tiles cool against my feet, and thrust my face towards the mirror. Pull my cheeks this way and that, examining the road map of scars and marks and freckles. I have new ones, postmarks of the Caribbean sun, taking over my nose and cheeks. Or maybe I can just see them better now I've lost weight. I'm thinner than I was before the wedding. Maybe the thinnest I've ever been. Practically translucent. I suck in my stomach and feel a familiar gnawing. I wonder what happiness tastes like, and if it's possible to be so completely alone that you can trick your body into feeling full.

Throughout the Instinctive Drowning Response, drowning people cannot voluntarily control their arm movements. When struggling on the surface of the water, drowning people cannot wave for help, move toward a rescuer or reach out for a piece of equipment.

"Are you sure this guy's legit?"

My husband glares suspiciously at Luis, who squints at the road from the driver's seat of his beaten-up old van. We bounce down a dirt track, flying over potholes and rubble, away from the city towards the coast. I don't say a thing as my head bumps against the head-rest of the seat in front. There are no safety belts. When we arrive at a small cove, Luis yanks on the hand-break and jumps out, singing a melody as he unloads gear from the boot. He looks up, arms full of breathing apparatus, and stops singing as he sees the dark clouds, as though he's worried the sky might break apart. I follow his frown to the shoreline. We'll go in, though, I'm sure of it. We've paid him the equivalent of a week's wages.

My husband doesn't notice my teeth chattering in the wind as we stand at the water's edge. He's too busy swearing as he wrestles with his snorkel. It's a little broken and I feel guilty for it, because it was my idea to come, because I know he hates it and we haven't even got our feet wet yet, because I carry guilt like an old lover I can't shake off. I do that thing I learned when I was a child, my 'special power'. If I hold my breath and sort of tense up my ears, I can blur out sound. Blur him out like he never existed, or I didn't.

My swimsuit snags on a rock. The cold water comes flooding in, making me gasp. A wave takes me by surprise and knocks me off my feet. Salt fills my nose and mouth. Luis waves to check I'm okay and I cough and wave back. My hair sticks to my face like snakes.

I can't help but think about that story I read about a lifeguard who rushed into the water to save a little girl from drowning, right in front of her oblivious parents. How easy it is to ignore signs of distress, even when they're right in front of you.

"Todo bien," I say, pinching my nose to get the water out.

"It is rough today," he replies in English. "But it is okay."

Luis mimes two hands around his eyes and I put on my mask. Three feet away I see my husband doing the same. I bite down on the mouthpiece of the snorkel, the bitter taste of rubber rough against my tongue. Underwater, sand swirls, wild and grainy.

From beginning to end of the Instinctive Drowning Response, people's bodies remain upright in the water, with no evidence of a supporting kick. Unless rescued by a trained lifeguard, drowning people can only struggle on the surface of the water from 20 to 60 seconds before submersion occurs.

By the time I realise what is happening, that he's gone out further than he should, swallowed too much water, it is already too late. My husband's face is the colour of concrete, eyes wide and white. I can't see his palms pushing down beneath the surface, asking for forgiveness, though I know they are there. Still, I don't move. Not even when I hear Luis shouting from the shore, the splash of his desperate strides. I have time, I think. Acres of time. Time to reflect, time to tread water, time where nothing is happening, not really. Except everything.

I still have a scar on my leg from the coral. You wouldn't know where it was unless you touched it – the skin rough where it should be smooth, faint lines where my blood turned toxic. You'd have to really know where to look to know it was ever there at all.

THE GIRL IN THE PHOTOGRAPH

It sits on the bookshelf, sandwiched between John Pilger and Koji Suzuki. It is small, no bigger than my hand, a wedge of brushed silver in a sea of black and orange manga spines. Its round eye gazes with cataract blindness across the empty living room. In its range of sight: the fireplace, framed in William Morris tiled brown, the armchair, the deep reds of the Persian rug.

Almost four years ago I lay spread-eagled across that carpet, pushed my fingers deep into its thick silk, rested my other hand on my swollen belly to trace the squirms. Now, parts of the rug are brushed the wrong way, permanently thickened by sticky fingers, food spillages and blobs of paint.

It's seen it all, the old Chinon 35EE. That first night home from the hospital, we were numbed into silence, nervously watching the love we'd created wrestle and writhe in a tiny Moses basket on the floor. We jumped up with every strangled cry; slept on our feet, standing, rocking. And that other, terrible night. A silent observer to the green uniforms of the paramedics, the steel glare of the oxygen canister, the rope, impossibly tight around his neck. The blue lights of the ambulance reflected in its passive lens.

Now, it lies partially obscured by a tall clock on a twisted metal stand, bearing Roman numerals I could never read, a gift from an aunt. The clock, too, lies in the dusky realms of the forgotten, time creaking slower as the batteries wear down. I've ignored the hour's change from summer to winter, despite the darkening windows, the streetlamps burning orange at four in the afternoon – five, if you go by the clock.

But today, on an unimportant Saturday, with the November rain keeping beat to the tinny tunes of the Disney film we've already watched twelve times or more, I remember. I've been scanning the bookshelf, searching for something to read. I'm looking for Norwegian Wood. I want to get lost in a world of wells, long walks, Tokyo jazz bars, cats and melancholy. Instead, I see the camera.

"Aha," I say out loud. Iris turns, one finger in her mouth. She is propped up on the floor, a pillow beneath her chin, her face less than a metre from the screen.

"What did you say, Mummy?"

I balance my mug of tea on the mahogany stool next to the sofa and stretch for it with one hand. "Nothing, darling, I was just surprised, that's all." I pick it up. It leaves a small square of dust like a saucer stain on the white wood of the middle shelf.

"Why were you surprised? What's that?"

I ignore her, turning it over to look at its narrow back, then over again. The lens is smudged, but not scratched. I shake it a little and it rattles. I can't remember putting it there. Could it have been when we first moved in, five years ago? Have I even used it, since?

Small fingers tug at my sleeve. Iris is on her feet, standing in front of me, dressed as Snow White. "What's that? What's that, Mummy? Is it a camera?"

"Yes, darling, but it's very old. Look –" I pull back the small silver handle on the top like I'm loading a catapult. Then I put the small viewing window to my eye and point it at Iris's face. I press the small button on the top. It makes a satisfying clicking sound, and she blinks.

"I just took your picture."

"Can I see?" she says, pushing her head against my chin. Her hair is in my mouth and I brush it away.

"It's not like the cameras you're used to." I turn it around to show her the back. "There's no screen, see? So we can't look at it. It's not like our phones."

"Oh," she's disappointed. "Why not? I want to see it, Mummy. I want to see the picture you took." She pulls on the small leather strap on its side.

"Careful!" I grab it before it falls to the floor, and smashes. "You have to be careful, Iris. It's old. It was Granddad's."

"Granddad's camera? Why? Did he give it to us?"

"He did," I say, frowning. I can't remember when, or why. "But it doesn't have a film in it yet. We'll need to buy one if we want to take real pictures. Look. The film goes in here."

I pry a tiny clasp on the camera's left side. It is sunk into another round dial. As I pull it, the whole dial lifts up to reveal a long screw. I pull a little harder, and the mechanical clasp on the side unlocks with a soft click. The back swings open. I regret it at once.

"What's wrong, Mummy? Why did you do that? Why did you shut it quickly?"

"Shit," I say, under my breath. "There *is* a film in it."

"You said the 'S' word!" Iris's eyes are agog. Then her attention turns back to the camera. "What does it mean, there's a film in it? What's a film?"

"Darling, hang on, please. Give me a minute." I want to scream. How could I be so stupid? Why did I assume it was empty? Anything that was on it now would be over-exposed, useless. There might have been photos of Tom on there. My heart hurts.

"What's the matter, Mummy?"

"Oh, Iris – it's nothing. It's okay. I opened the back of the camera because I thought it was empty, but there was a film in there. Did you see? The black, shiny stuff – like paper. But if you open a camera when there's a film in it then you won't be able to see the pictures, because films don't like the light."

"How do we see the pictures?"

I sigh, push the dial back into itself, flap the clasp down on the top. I squeeze the back of the camera together tightly, put it face-down into my lap, to give it darkness, as if that will help. I turn the handle on the other side, back and forth, until it won't turn anymore.

"I think," I start the process all over again: lift up the tiny clasp, lift the dial up with it, pull harder, wait for the click and the release of the main hinge, "this might wind up the film – like – this." I take a deep breath and open the back of the camera, let it out again with a whistle.

"Phew," I say, smiling for the first time. Iris looks at my face, her eyes inscrutable. They're so dark they're almost black. She wrinkles her nose. "Is it ok, Mummy? Is it brokened?"

"Nope, see?" I prise it out with my fingernail and hold it up for her to see. "This is a film."

38

"What do we do with it?"

"Well, on Monday we'll take it to the pharmacy and they'll take it away and turn it into pictures for us."

"Will we be able to look at them tomorrow?"

"Not tomorrow, darling."

"Oh... I want to look at them tomorrow."

"Don't pout," I reach out and stroke the soft skin beneath her chin. She turns her head away crossly, and I stroke her hair. "We have to be patient. It takes a few days. It'll be a surprise."

She folds her arms across her chest. "I want to look at them tomorrow," she says, stamping her foot. Her hair catches the light and shines like a halo. It always takes me aback, how different we look – her blonde hair contrasting with my red, her olive skin dark against my pale freckles. If you saw us in the street you wouldn't even think she was mine. Though Mum and Dad said that she was the image of me when I was her age, that if nothing else, she has my eyes. Funny how much we change.

Sunday blooms. My parents visit, something they've done without fail since the funeral. "Look over there, Dad," I say, pointing to the third shelf. I've wiped away the dust, rubbed the fingermarks from the lens with a soft cloth. "Recognise that?"

"What's that?" he frowns, looking up over his half-moon lenses. "Is that my old camera? When did that become yours, then?"

In an instant I'm a teenager again. "You gave it to me years ago!"

"Does it still work?" He stands, wincing as his knee pops, grabs it, sits back down next to me on the sofa. "Chinon 35EE," he says, turning it over to inspect it. "Good camera, this. Took it with me on my travels."

I could listen to tales of Dad's travels in the 1970s for hours. My favourite is the one about the time he smuggled himself across Afghanistan in the back of a chicken truck, and the time he worked as a waiter in Tehran. I'd hoped some of those shots, of a life so distant it would feel like ghosts, would be on the camera. And now I'd opened it and ruined them all.

"I didn't know there was a film in there," I said gloomily. "I opened it, yesterday, with Iris. I closed it again, straight away, but it'll be too late, won't it? To see anything? I might take it in anyway, to get developed…."

"I wouldn't bother," Dad frowns, putting the camera down on the arm of the sofa. "It'll be over-exposed. Be lucky if you get more than a white glare."

"I'm so annoyed with myself." I pull at my bottom lip. "Any idea what could've been on there? I can't remember the last time I used it."

"No idea. I didn't even know you had it."

Monday beckons, bringing with it the usual rush: pick up groceries, return Iris's books to the library, pay our weekly fine. It's only as we pass the pharmacy that I remember it, small and shiny black at the bottom of my bag.

"Do you even take these, anymore?" I joke to the sales assistant as she takes the film from me. She can't be more than eighteen. She probably hasn't ever used a disposable camera at a wedding, or cringed at end-of-the-night shots of smudged make-up, terrible outfits and mistaken kisses. She ignores my question and writes me a receipt, tells me it'll be ready by Friday.

The week passes in a blur of work and nursery drop-offs; fielding calls from concerned friends in the evenings, when Iris finally goes to sleep. "You should date," they tell me. "Get back out there." I laugh them off – tell them the only love in my life is the one upstairs, snoring in a Gruffalo sleep-suit.

At the back of my mind, the film lurks constantly, dark and tantalising. But by Friday, it's slipped. It's a busy day at the shop and it's only as I'm walking home through the shadowy park that I realise I was meant to pick it up. *Shit.* I check my watch, but it's gone six, too late. Damn. It'll have to wait, again. Something to brighten the weekend, with its usual ups and downs. I'll do as I always do; try to keep us busy, out of the house, so I don't notice the silence too much: ballet, brunch with friends, play-dates. Football on in the afternoon, with nobody to watch it.

"What are we doing tomorrow, Mummy?" Iris asks, fighting to keep her eyes open, as I tuck her into bed. "I'm not at nursery, am I?"

"Not tomorrow," I whisper, kissing the peach fuzz of her cheek, breathing in her milky scent. "Tomorrow is Saturday." I stroke the side of her face and am filled with the dizzying urge to bite down into her soft flesh. "We'll do something fun, I promise. After we've picked up those photos, from Granddad's old camera."

"I want to look at the photographs," she says, yawning widely. "I want to see the pictures of me on there."

"Well, just that one," I say, stifling a smile. "The rest will be too old. Go to sleep now."

"I love you, Mummy," she murmurs. I stand and make for the door. "Hey!" she says. "You have to say, 'I love you too'!"

"I love you too. Now go to sleep." She's gone before I can even finish my sentence. I go into the bedroom and flop down on the bed. I bite a nail that's torn and sharp and stare at the ceiling. I think for a moment of looking at porn, of watching something to turn me on, but know it'll just leave me dissatisfied. I stretch out my foot. The sheets are cold and empty.

The next day, we're up at 6am, eating breakfast, watching TV. Around 10am, we finally leave the house. It's cold out and the frost stings my cheeks. Iris shouts Disney songs at the top of her lungs as she scoots along. Every time we get close to a busy road, my heart leaps into my throat and I lunge forward, convinced she won't stop. But she always does.

"You mustn't go so fast, Iris – it's dangerous!"

"Sorry, Mummy," she yells, screeching off at full pelt. Eventually, we make it to the pharmacy. The same girl is behind the counter. She looks bored.

"I'm here to pick up a film," I pant, eyes scanning the aisles for Iris. I see the handles of her scooter vanish as she makes for the rice cakes and gummy vitamins.

"Name?" the girl barks. I tell her and wait as she thumbs through packs of blue envelopes with manicured nails. Iris rolls towards me, clutching five packets of super-plus extra tampons. "I found these, Mummy!" she crows. "Can we get them?"

"No, we can't – thanks." I take the packet from the girl and put it in my bag. I pay, grab the long strap attached to the scooter and wheel Iris out of the door.

We get home at lunchtime, after a mandatory tour of the swings, slide and the library, and it's only once we're nestled on the sofa together, my arm around her waist, that I remember.

"Oh yeah!" I jump up and go out to the hall.

"Why did you say, "Oh yeah?"" Her voice is faint from behind the living room door.

I push the door open and sit back down next to Iris. I rip open the packet and take out the inner envelope, *Let's feel good* printed on its sleeve.

I take out the first photograph, and my heart sinks. "Oh no, Granddad was right..." It's nothing but a gradient of colour, from white to yellow, orange to blue, against a black background. The images within are too blurred, too out of focus to be clear enough to make out. The next is the same, and the next. But then –

"Is that my daddy?' Iris asks, and my heart contracts, suddenly and sharply.

"Yes," I say, stroking her curls, staring at his profile. He had such a handsome profile. "Do you remember him?"

"A bit," she says, peering at it. "He had to go, didn't he?"

"Well," I frown. "I don't know about that. But he's gone now, yes."

"And we won't ever see him again," Iris repeats with a grin, in a silly, singsong voice.

"Well, no. But it's a sad thing, Iris." I look at her, trying to make her understand. "It's not funny. It's sad when someone dies. Especially when you love them very much."

"Bye bye," she repeats, staring down at the photograph. I wonder if I should be worried. The counsellor said children deal with grief in different ways, that she may start acting out, talking about him a lot – or not at all. Death is 'too arbitrary for children to understand', she said. Instinctively, I glance over at the armchair, now piled high with cushions and magazines. I know I'll never sit there again. Not in his chair.

"Let's look at some more pictures, Mummy." Iris is getting restless. I move the one of him to the back of the pile, let out an involuntary yelp when I see what's beneath it.

"Is that your pussycat?" Iris asks.

"Yep. That's Smokey. He was lovely. He used to sleep on my bed every night. I told him all my secrets."

"Where is he now?"

"Well, he died," I say, watching her warily. Perhaps too much talk of death would make things worse? "He was very old."

Iris frowns, puts the photo next to her on the sofa. There's another shot of Smokey, in his favourite spot beneath the radiator in the house I grew up in.

44

"Hang on, darling!"

Iris has begun impatiently shuffling through the photographs, knocking a couple of them to the floor.

"What are you doing? I want to look at these properly, please. Iris, stop!"

I reach down to pick them up. The first makes me smile – it was taken from my old bedroom window. My brother is outside with one of his friends at an ice-cream van. He looks young, no older than fourteen. Now he's thirty-one, and getting married.

"Look, Iris," I breathe. "It's Uncle Jack." Unbelievable – that means some of the shots on this film are at least seventeen years old.

"He's got funny hair!" she giggles, pointing at his bleached spikes, another photo clutched in her hand. "I like this one, Mummy." She shoves it at my chest.

I smooth it out, look at it. It's a beach. I don't remember it at first, until I spot myself, dressed in black, hood up, sunglasses on, headphones in my ears. Ah, yes. The family holiday that signalled the end of family holidays.

Iris spots me. "Who's that?"

"That's Mummy," I say, looking at Iris. I wonder if she'll be as teenaged and difficult as I was. It seems inevitable.

"And that's me!" Iris beams, pointing to a child in the background.

"No, that's not you."

She stamps her foot.

"Darling, I'm sorry, but it's not you. Look — that's Mummy, and I was very young then. I think I was only sixteen. So that can't be you, can it? You weren't even born, then."

"It *is* me," she pouts. "Look."

I sigh. It does look like her, though the child is bending over, building sandcastles. It's hard to see her face but she has the same, sun-streaked blonde hair, the same skin. Even the bridge of her nose, which wrinkles as she focuses on the task at hand, is strangely similar.

"Oh yes," I frown. "That little girl does look a bit like you. But it's not you, sweetheart. That little girl must be... well, a grown-up, by now. She might even have a little girl of her own!"

"But I remember," Iris wails. "I remember Granddad losing his flip-flop in the water."

I laugh, because I remember too. Dad was so annoyed, he insisted on wading into the sea to get it, even after high-tide, even after the lifeguards on the beach told him it wasn't safe. We must have talked about it in front of Iris. It was incredible what she remembered.

There I am at university in the next photograph, nineteen or so, sporting dreadlocks and a nose ring. In the next, I'm outside our student house in the street, jumping high into the air. It's snowing and someone has written 'poo' on the window of a green Ford Ka parked in the street.

"Look," Iris said. "That's me. See?"

"Hmmm? No, sweetie, that's Mummy, being silly..."

"No, look," Iris tugs at my sleeve. She points with a chipped, bright pink fingernail to the window of the house in the foreground of the shot. "There I am!"

Goosebumps spread across my cheek and the back of my neck. On the second floor of the house, a little girl presses her face against the window. Her eyes are dark, her hair fair and bobbed. She has olive skin, and a perfect circle has formed from the condensation on the glass. She stares directly into the lens, without smiling.

"That's strange. She *does* look like you."

"It *is* me, Mummy," Iris says softly. "I told you."

I bite my lip and move the photograph hurriedly to the back. The next is a forest scene. It's snowing again, the ground covered in footprints, but we've jumped back in time. I'm tiny. I'm staring at the camera, a solemn expression on my face. There's a woman a few metres away from me, watching me and smiling. She must be out for a walk with her family on the same day. My dad is almost out of shot, and he's turned to the side, talking to someone – probably my mum. His hair is a light brown, rather than grey. He has a beard. He looks so young. The photos must have been mixed up when they were developed. And this same roll of film must stretch across more than thirty years, not just seventeen.

But – wait. I grab the photo and bring it closer to my face. My hand shakes. What's going on? Is this some kind of joke?

"I like that snowsuit, Mummy. It's my favourite. But it's a bit small for me."

Iris has her hands tucked into her armpits, showing me where it's tight.

"That's not you, darling, it's Mummy." I swallow, hard. It *has* to be me. Though... I don't remember Dad having a beard. I fish my mobile phone out of my pocket, search for 'Dad' and press 'dial' with a shaking hand.

"Everything ok?" he booms, answering after a few rings.

"Yes, fine." I nibble a nail and watch Iris. She picks up a doll from the floor and plays with it, unbuttons the doll's coat and redoes it, murmurs made-up conversations in which she's the mother and 'has to go to work now'.

"Hi, Dad." The words catch in my throat. I know how stupid this is going to sound. "I got those photos developed, the ones from your old camera."

"Oh yes, how were they? Any of them come out?"

"Quite a few, actually. But I just wanted to ask you something – there's a shot of us in the forest, as a family, I mean. You look pretty young, I mean, you've got a beard! But I don't... well, I don't remember you, with a beard. When did you shave it off?"

I hear a scratching noise as he rubs his stubbly chin with his hand. "A beard? I only had a beard once, for about a year, I think, before your mum made me shave it off."

I'm flooded with relief. "Ha, that sounds about right."

"I got rid of it right before we got married," Dad carries on. "She was worried about how I'd look in the wedding photos. Yep, that's right. So I suppose that was... well, we've just had our 39th wedding anniversary – so it must have been about... '79, I think."

48

I nearly drop the phone. "'79? You mean, 1979?" The hairs on my arms stand on end. I say a hurried goodbye, hang up and look at the picture again, at the little girl I thought was me. The hood of her snowsuit, pulled tight at the neck; the stray strands of hair, strands I'd assumed were red – but could be blonde. Could be. I squint and look at them again, turn the photo from side-to-side in my hand. I look at her eyes.

I rummage through the others with shaking hands, flicking past blurred lines, blurred faces, until I come to the last few. Until I see Tom.

The expression on his face – his eyes wide, his skin pale and gaunt – chills me to the core. He's looking into the lens; Iris frozen in time behind him, her hands outstretched. He's holding the camera out in front of him to capture the two of them together. He looks afraid, his mouth frozen in a silent scream.

Then I turn to the last photograph, the one I took little more than a week ago; of Iris, in her Snow White costume. I compare it to the others: Iris, at the beach, Iris at the window of a house, Iris, in the forest – photographs ten, twenty, even thirty years old. It's impossible. She's only four. Isn't she?

I drop them to the floor and look over at my daughter. She sits comfortably in her dad's armchair, facing the bookshelf, gazing into the dark and unflinching lens of the camera. It reflects her olive skin, her eyes – *my* eyes – so brown they're almost black. She stares at it for a long, long time, without blinking. She smiles.

AND THE WORLD WAS WATER

It takes three days for the waves to reach the tenth storey.

His arm is a solid comfort across my back. We lay on our fronts, the sharp scratch of tarmac against our chins, gazing over the lip of the tower block. It doesn't seem so high anymore. I guess it isn't. Not now the first 150 feet or so are submerged in a mass of murky green-grey. Seaweed clings to the outside of the windows, dried and braided like snakes.

"How long do you think —"

Another pointless question. One or the other of us has been saying the same thing in myriad ways since we first ran up here, via the fire escape twisted in a helter-skelter frown. The scratches we carved like bruises into metal to mark where the water first licked the sides disappeared two days ago. The steps have vanished, too. It's only another couple of feet until it reaches the top, which means us. Our sanctuary. 'Home'. The only wedding chapel we'll ever know.

"A few days?" he says, with so much of a pause I'd almost forgotten I'd spoken. I nod, sigh a little. Rub my foot lazily against his.

The air is warm and stuffy. Has been since the water levels started to rise. As though we were encased in a bubble or a small room, or in one of those war films, where people get trapped inside a submarine. Something always seems to appear to save them, though. An air vent. A door yanked open suddenly from the outside. Nobody would be yanking any doors open to save us anytime soon. There weren't any doors to yank. Or people.

We hadn't been quite so alone when we first got here. For a while, we could wave and other scattered survivors would wave back from the tops of buildings close enough (though not actually close enough) to jump. We were alone now, though. Most of those who'd begun waving, cheerily enough, probably hadn't thought to move supplies up to the roof with them, like we had. Though even ours were running short. We still had dried meat and a few tins and two barrels of whiskey: liquid gold. They'd been here when we arrived, of course. There's no way we could've lugged them up here, all by ourselves. When the day came, we'd sworn to drink it all and go out in a fog of sleep, wrapped around each other tight as the old couple found in bed in the Titanic.

I move my chin and rest my cheek against the rough concrete. Before the tides came, I used to stand at the edge of a building like this, right at the top, and assess the likelihood of dying by falling. I didn't want to just break a couple of limbs; to inconvenience my life like that. I didn't want to spend a couple of weeks in hospital, or be sponge-bathed by nurses because my wrists and ankles were covered in plaster. I wanted my skull to crack and ooze like grapefruit. It wouldn't do that now, though, anyway. We probably weren't even high enough; not anymore, even though we were at the very top of what used to be one of the tallest residential buildings in London. Water only resembles concrete – is as hard, as devastating – if you get about 250 feet above it. And 250 feet equates to roughly 20 to 25 storeys in a building, depending on the height of one storey, according to the internet. Which doesn't exist either, anymore. Not now the cables are all wet.

Telecommunications went down on the day of the most terrible storm anyone had ever known. Huge cracks of lightning as pylons hit the water; as sparks flew, as vast swathes of the city turned black as coal. The bodies began to rise to the surface a few hours later. Poor bastards trapped in basements, stuffing meat into machines in factories, chemicals staining their fingers. They went first. Since then, we'd grown almost used to the odd cadaver floating by. Had developed a certain... gallows humour about it. Gave them names. Jobs. Personalities. We imagined them in bed, bestowed them with weird kinks. We called them 'floaters'.

"Timothy," he says now, nudging me in the ribs as a huge floater drifts by, face down, a tuft of grey hair sticking up like a sail. "Worked in a library. Told any attractive woman who came in that his favourite writer was Simone de Beauvoir. Actually read Dan Brown. Liked picking earwax and sniffing it. His own, of course. Timothy was no monster."

I elbow him back. "Grim," I said. "Not Dan Brown. Stephen King. Timothy had taste – and not just for earwax."

I roll on to my side and shuffle a couple of inches closer to bury my face in his neck. I want to hide from it all. Stay here, right here, breathing him in. With my eyes closed I can almost imagine us 'normal'. Everyday lovers, sleeping in late on a Sunday morning. Biting deep into a basket of fresh fruit: pears and papayas and ripe, swollen mangoes; letting the juice run down our chins. Squinting at each other in a haze of half-sleep, dizzy with soft-focus smiles and sex and wanting and time. Time. The one thing we don't have. Not now we're the last two people alive in a man-made apocalypse.

And it was man-made, as far as we can tell. The initial reports sounded like any others. 'Freak weather' branding; talk of sandbags and stockpiling and old air raid shelters. 'Flood horror' screamed the tabloids. 'Thousands predicted DEAD. Millions of homes WIPED OUT.' Scaremongering, in predictable caps lock.

We'd rolled our eyes and gone back to the broadsheets, which told a muted version of the same story, written from the told-you-so perspective of climate change. Homes from Cornwall to Middlesborough at risk with eighty flood warnings and one hundred and sixty-two flood alerts. A deluge of rain battering the south of England. Firemen forced to rescue twenty people after torrential rain devastated their homes. Thick fog and icy roads leading to a sixty-nine-car pile-up. Rivers bursting their banks in Kent, East Sussex and Berkshire. Unsettled weather, heavy rain and strong winds. A tornado hitting the Surrey town of Chertsey, stripping tiles from rooftops. The Met Office took to Twitter to post photos of the damage; circled areas on Doppler images highlighting what they called 'rapid circulation'.

It was worse than any of that, of course. Worse than any of us could have imagined. We should have paid more attention to the birds, for they felt it first. They'd been growing in number, pecking at the patches of algae that had started to appear, moving nests, busying themselves in frantic, twig-by-twig industry. We were too busy measuring what was left of the horizon to register the creeping sea of black all around us, the oil slick of feathers. By the time we saw – *really* saw – it was already too late. Humanity drowned out in an ecstasy of cawing.

"Do you remember what a peach tastes like?"

I smile sideways. "A peach?"

"A peach," he repeats. "My mum used to buy us peaches at the local grocer that were shaped like bottoms – sort of flat around the sides, slightly square. My sister and I would tease each other to eat the 'bum peach'. We found it hilarious. Sort of disgusting, but hilarious. It always tasted so sweet."

"What about brie, though?"

He grimaces. "Are you mad? Peaches and brie do *not* go together."

"I know that." I give him my best eye-roll. "I didn't mean with the peach – though come on, cheese and grapes? Fruit and cheese *always* go together."

He shifts and stretches his back until it cracks. Nods.

"When I was a kid I was obsessed with brie," I say absently and, as I do, I'm eight again, and in my mother's kitchen. Treading carefully over the mint-green lino, sticky with mud from the garden. Celine Dion belting a ballad from the old-fashioned dial radio in the corner. My mother humming along, her hands full of ironing. Next to her on the wall is her favourite calendar: Kevin Costner, permanently stuck in 1998. She liked him best, then.

"You were obsessed with brie, when you were a kid?" He's teasing. I can tell without looking at his face that the corners of his mouth are turned up like commas, curved and beautiful. "Did you have gout while all the other kids had chicken-pox?"

"Shut up!" I dig my finger into his ribs. "It was the best thing I'd ever tasted, *actually*. I used to put it in a bowl in the microwave to melt it, then eat it with a spoon."

He shakes his head slowly. "That is genuinely the most disturbing thing I've ever heard."

"...says the man stranded on the top of a skyscraper with someone he's only known for days, but is definitely going to die with?"

He reaches round to my side and pulls me in close until I can feel the rise and fall of his breathing against my ribs.

"....says the man stranded on the top of a skyscraper with someone he's only known for days, but feels like he's known forever, who he is definitely going to die with. Yes. You disturb me."

He bends his head down to kiss me. He tastes of whiskey and salt.

"What else do you miss?" I murmur, pulling away to look at him. His eyes are the same shade of mossy green as the algae that clings to the surface of everything around us. "The little things. Tell me, so I can remember them too. Taste them."

"Ice cream," he says immediately. "Vanilla ice cream — so cold it hurts your teeth and gives you brain freeze; so rich it tastes like clotted cream." He sits up, suddenly. "No, wait!"

I feign shock, clutch at my chest.

"Actual clotted cream," he says, as seriously as if he were a doctor with bad news to import. "With a *hot mince pie*." This last part, he whispers. Then he closes his eyes and drops back again to the floor. Begins rolling from side to side, as though wracked with pain.

"I can taste it," he groans. "Smell it. It almost hurts."

I can smell it, too; my mouth metallic with wanting. Cinnamon and cardamom and the sharp scissor-scent of oranges. Mulled wine, rolling crimson in a metal pot on the hob. Ginger wine burning the back of my throat with its sticky sweetness. Rare roast beef and potatoes and bread sauce and —

"Stop." I clap my hands over my mouth. "It's... too much."

Too late. Images flood my mind like a photograph of the last Christmas I can remember. My stomach twists and writhes. Seawater floods my open mouth. I swallow it shut.

"Christmas... pudding," I sigh.

"Stollen," he says wistfully.

"Cranberry sauce."

"Stuffing."

"Brussel sprouts."

I nod, ignoring his quizzical eyebrows. "Yep. *Even* Brussel sprouts. Sautéed with bacon and walnuts." I close my eyes and see steaming plates, piled high on my mother's wooden table. "Cold roast beef and mashed potato — smothered in butter — and gravy. Lashings of gravy." I can't stop talking. My tongue is moving faster than my lips, tripping over the words. "I'm talking boatfuls of dark, thick gravy that sloshes against the sides of the plate like it's gonna throw you overboard —"

He lets out a sudden yell of frustration, cutting me dead. His voice bounces off the glass and chrome of the office block next to us, before getting sucked into the hot concrete of our small, square surrounds. When we first discovered we were stuck up here, we yelled a lot. Every time we did, we held each other, suspended in nervous silence; listening out for a returning call. All we ever heard were echoes.

The spell is broken. The food disappears. The sky begins to darken to give way to another night, another rough night. We gaze again at the water below us, almost close enough to touch.

"What will we do, when it comes?"

I speak but don't speak. My teeth graze his skin. I press them there, harder, to leave a mark that can't be washed away.

"Swim," he says. The first time he's answered. Really answered. "As long and as fast as we can."

"To where? There's nowhere left."

He is silent. Then he shifts and stares at me, fierce and direct. Grips my hand so hard it hurts.

"Anywhere. Nowhere. We don't have to know where we're going until we get there. But we *will* get there."

I stare back, and know I would have loved him even if we hadn't met this way; if we hadn't been the last two people left. That, in in the end, it doesn't matter anyway. And for a moment – here, now, his hand in mine – I can't even hear the water.

TSURIS

The receptionist pointed to a dark wooden door. Was it pulsing? It looked like it was pulsing. Sara swallowed, but her mouth was dry and it made her gag. She forced herself to take a deep breath – in through her mouth, out through her nose – then walked to the door with slow, hesitant steps and knocked. Her knuckles grazed slightly against its rough surface.

"Come in!" It was a female voice. Sara hesitated, wondering if it was too late to run. What if someone had seen her? What if an acquaintance had tried to catch up with her in the street, to ask her how preparations were coming along for *Pesach*? What if their eyes had strayed to 'Forest Counselling' on the small sign on the wall outside, so they'd shrunk back and watched her go in alone? Who might they tell?

"Come in," the voice called again, interrupting her panic. Sara placed her hand on the warm brass. She tugged at the sleeves of her shirt, dragging them down to cover her fingers.

The first thing she saw in the room was a menacing mahogany desk, bare, save for a large red notebook and a box of tissues. A woman was behind it, and she was luminous. Her strong nose shone in the dusty light overhead, her teeth startlingly straight, her hair a glossy black. She smiled and gestured for Sara to take a seat. As she did so, her eyes momentarily flicked to the floor where Sara stood. *Ugh.* What would this glorious woman make of... well, this?

Sara looked down too at her scuffed and battered old shoes, her baggy tights, the hair beneath course and curling and achingly visible. 'Natural tan', they called the colour of these tights. There was nothing natural about it. Sara reached down to tug at the hem of her skirt. It felt tight across her swollen belly, clung uncomfortably to her bottom. It was itchy – wool, of course, the only material that seemed to be available in the shops round here, even though it was April and the rest of London had bare shoulders, uncovered ankles and slick collarbones.

Sara pulled out the wooden chair gratefully and dropped her handbag to the floor, nudging it out of sight with her foot. Tissues exploded on the carpet like fireworks – some clean, mostly dirty – pooling next to half-eaten snacks left by the kids, an apple core, toys and a stack of papers. Sara was in charge of collecting funds for next year's charitable trip to Poland. She hadn't got more than a dozen names though, yet, and it wasn't enough. Lately she'd just been too... distracted.

Sara shrugged out of her jacket, her eyes meeting the counsellor's before flicking away. She hoped she didn't look as nervous as she felt. She crossed her feet at the ankles and then changed her mind, crossing them at the knee instead, but that hitched her skirt up a couple of inches and revealed the hairs on her legs, so she uncrossed them again.

"I'm Deborah," the woman said, her voice rich and welcoming. "But please, call me Debbie."

Sara couldn't help gazing at her mouth, which was a deep pink, and split a little in the middle at the bottom. It looked sore, and Sara momentarily wanted to reach out and touch it.

"Is it okay to call you Sara?"

Sara nodded, biting her own lip. She had a disorientating sense of seeing herself through Debbie's eyes. What must she look like? A twenty-something woman in an ill-fitting hairpiece, the threadbare scalp showing through to the netting, the colour a shade too severe for her pale skin. *Sheitels* were so expensive, these days – more than £1,000 for real human hair. There was no way they could afford that, not with Avi on a trainee Rabbi's wage and her looking after the kids full-time.

"Let me just talk you through a bit of house-keeping, Sara," Debbie said, her hands spread out over the surface of the desk. Sara felt a buzzing sensation somewhere inside her as Debbie explained that she might take notes from time to time, but that everything she told her would be confidential – unless she had reason to believe Sara was a 'danger' to herself or to others.

Sara sat straight up in her chair. Dangerous? To whom, her kids? She would never hurt them – never! She opened her mouth, prepared to make her excuses to leave, but Debbie's smile blinded her and she couldn't think straight. She sat on her hands. Felt the outline of her wedding band sharp and cold against her thigh.

"Shall we get started?" Debbie wore a simple white shirt. Beneath it was a glint of gold, and Sara thought she saw a cross nestled at the soft dip at the base of her throat. She was glad that Debbie might be a Christian, despite the differences between them that would throw up. More than if she'd professed no interest in religion whatsoever.

Sara closed her eyes for a moment and tried to refocus on her breathing. Her mind felt curiously empty; her mouth, more so. In the half-light at 4am this morning, Avi snoring on the other side of the room, Sara had pictured herself striding in here and unburdening herself entirely, not caring what she said or what anyone else thought. Now, she couldn't imagine saying a single word.

"What brings you here today, Sara?"

Sara opened her eyes. She ran her tongue over her lips. They felt dusty.

Debbie's voice was gentle. "In your own time."

Her stomach churned. Nobody would believe she was here, nobody. Yet, here she was, talking to a stranger – a *goy*, of all things.

"Umm," Sara said. "Well. The thing is... I've been having... *unnatural thoughts.*" This last part, she whispered.

"Unnatural thoughts?" Debbie repeated. "Can you tell me what that means?"

Sara cringed. How on earth to explain it? Her hand on the soft curve of her stomach in the grey dawn, wandering down below the covers. Gently, quietly, in case the rustle of the bedsheets woke Avi. Her eyes, half-closed. A smile on her lips. Her mouth silently calling out *that* name.

Sara clasped her hands together, wringing them like she was squeezing out a wet towel. It felt so much worse to bring her terrible secret to life in the presence of somebody else. She waited for Debbie to read her mind, to admonish her, to tell her she shouldn't be thinking of anything but being a good wife.

"Sara," Debbie said softly. "Are you talking about sex? Sexual thoughts?"

Sara reeled backwards as if she'd been hit. "Don't say it, please!" she blurted out, her hands out in front of her in protection. "It is not *right!*"

"I'm sorry," Debbie said immediately. "But this is a safe space, Sara. I'm here to help you."

Sara rocked slightly, staring again at the damp patch on the ceiling. She felt the hot sting of tears behind her eyes and sent out a quick prayer to *Hashem* to forgive her. Her stomach squirmed and she didn't know if it was the baby or her own discomfort. This was a mistake.

"Sara," Debbie said then. "What makes you so sure they're unnatural?"

Sara stopped, halfway into the sleeve of her jacket. She looked across the desk at Debbie. "I'm married," she said. "Ten years, now. My husband is due to take his exams. To become a Rabbi." She paused, then forced it out. She was doomed anyway. *Hashem* knew everything. "I've been having... thoughts. About a *woman.*"

"Okay," Debbie said simply. "What kind of thoughts?"

Sara couldn't help it. Her mind flashed instantly to her studies all those years ago in Jerusalem at the all-female *midrasha,* to the roommate she'd been assigned – to Rebecca. The scent of her perfume on the pillow, the aching softness of her skin. The way her thighs rippled with goosebumps in the breeze from the open window in the small room they shared. Sara could hear Rebecca's terrible singing in the shower, smell the coconut shampoo she used, hear herself shrieking, "Stop!" as they rolled around between their twin beds, tickling and laughing until they could no longer breathe. She saw the curve of her lips, felt their wetness against hers. She shook her head. Ran her hands once more over her swollen belly.

"When is your baby due?" Debbie gestured to her stomach and smiled.

Sara was grateful for the distraction. "Three months."

"And do you have any other children?"

Sara nodded. "Asher, Lauren and Moshe." *Baruch Hashem*, she added silently, under her breath. Thanks be to G-d.

"How old are they?"

"Five, three and one."

"That can't be easy."

Sara shrugged and attempted a small smile, then looked around the room, anywhere but at Debbie. There was a sorry-looking plant in the corner, its leaves coated in dust and straggled with split ends. They'd once had an old family cat which used to chew languidly on flowing, ponytail palms like that. It would get bits stuck in its throat and squat on the floor, hackles high, neck bobbed low, as it wheezed and hacked. Sara and her sisters used to jump up in a panic when it first began doing it, convinced it was choking to death. But whatever it had consumed – hair, grass, secrets, those leaves – always came out eventually.

"Let me ask you a question, Sara," Debbie said. Her voice was smooth and steady. "Have you spoken to anyone else about this? A family member, perhaps? A friend?"

Sara was startled. "No," she spluttered. "Of course not!"

"And why is that?"

"Because then they'd *know*."

"Know what?"

"Everything!"

The thought of talking to someone – anyone – in her community about this… it was impossible. And she didn't have any friends outside. That was the reason she'd come to Forest in the first place.

"I think I understand," Debbie said. "Sara – what happens in your community, when someone wants to be with someone of the same sex? I imagine it's hard for them."

That was an understatement. Just look at Naomi.

Naomi was one of the teenagers who used to come to Sara and Avi's house, once a month, for one of Sara's 'girls' nights', in her unofficial role as *Rebbetzen* and guidance counsellor. Sara loved those nights. She'd spend ages preparing treats for them: manicures, face masks, scented candles. Then she'd read them some scripture on Jewish women's roles and duties and field any questions they might have. Much of the time it was about getting married. As a married woman she was best-placed to advise them on how to get a good match, probably a boy from the *yeshiva*. They wanted to know so much: about the *mikveh*, about the wedding night, about what happened when you were bleeding. Some of the girls were converts, but most had grown up in religious families and had mothers and sisters who had been through it, so it wasn't completely alien to them. Naomi was one of those girls. Sara could well imagine how terrible she must've felt, mustering up the courage to ask Sara if she could speak to her alone.

"I knew a girl," Sara said suddenly, looking at Debbie. "Naomi. She was fourteen when she came to me. She told me she was confused, that she thought she was in love. When I asked her who with, she said it was with her best friend." Sara swallowed. "A girl. I told her she had a choice – to follow that path alone, or to get married and raise a family. She chose to have a family. For us... there is no other option."

"I see. And this woman you have feelings for," Debbie said. "Is she someone you still see?"

Sara shook her head. "It was a long time ago," she said. She fanned her face with her hand. Why was it so hot? "Before I was married. I was a student."

"Are you still in touch?"

Sara's heart contracted painfully as she slowly shook her head. She'd stopped replying to Rebecca's emails shortly after her parents had whisked her home to meet her match. Avi was the son of one of her father's clients. Tall, nice-looking, with a degree in economics. She had no idea where Rebecca was now, what she was doing, whether she was married. She couldn't imagine Rebecca married.

"My husband is a good man," Sara said.

She pressed her fingers to her eyes, massaging the space between her brows. She'd slept badly last night, again. Avi had lain like a stone as usual, oblivious to her tossing and turning. She welcomed the gap between their beds. It gave her space to think, to make room for the fear which settled around her in the darkness like a duvet. She couldn't bear the thought of him trying to touch her like he was trying to fumble his way into an old coat.

"It sounds like quite some time has passed," Debbie said. "What made you decide to come and talk to someone about this now?"

Sara put her hand to her belly and felt the baby move. How to explain how she'd been feeling since she found out she was expecting again? Throughout her marriage Sara had never felt very sexual, had convinced herself she had a low libido, but carried on making love to Avi nonetheless – it was a *mitzvah,* after all. Yet since she'd been pregnant this time her dreams had been more vivid than ever before, and every one of them centred around Rebecca. When she awoke each morning alone, flushed and tingling, she found herself cycling all too rapidly from satisfaction, to hope, to disappointment.

"I keep thinking about her," Sara said, resigned to her confession. "I don't know why. I'll be walking along the street and see someone in the distance that looks a bit like her. But by the time I catch up to them I realise it's not her at all."

She bit her finger, picked at a loose bit of nail. "I keep wondering what she's doing, whether she's living a religious life. It was hard for her."

It wasn't just hard for Rebecca – it was impossible. Sara almost mustered a smile as she remembered the scowl on Rebecca's face as she was ordered to cover up in the searing Middle East heat; as the *madrachot* explained it was 'right' and 'proper' for observant women to wear long skirts – never trousers, for that would show off the outline of their bodies. She could practically hear Rebecca's quiet seething on their organised trips into the ultra-orthodox neighbourhood of *Meah Shearim*, her hissed outrage at the signs painted on walls commanding women to "wear modest clothes", her harrumphing at the *madrachot's* warnings to look at the floor when passing groups of *Hassidic* men in long, black fur coats and bearskin hats.

Rebecca had grown up with three brothers, close to the beach on the outskirts of Los Angeles. She resented anything that stopped her playing cricket, riding bikes and surfing and was in Israel as a last resort – her parents determined to instil in her some piety and some direction. She had cried when they dropped her off at the airport.

"She was never quite sure, Rebecca." Sara looked over her shoulder at the door. She had a sudden and irrational fear someone might be listening.

"But you were?"

Sara nodded. Wasn't it obvious? She was the daughter of a Rabbi. She had worn long socks and long skirts since she was five years old. She didn't remember seeing her mother wearing anything but a wig except when they were at home alone, when she'd take it off and brush out her long hair.

Debbie wouldn't understand – or could she? Was *her* family full of sadness? Did her grandfather, like Sara's – long since passed, *alav ha-sholom* – have tears in his eyes every time he talked of the past? "I have many regrets," he would tell them. "*Tsuris.*" His voice would crack as he recalled ghosts.

How could she possibly explain what it was like being the youngest in a family of six children, of sharing a room with her middle sister, Chana? How she flushed as she pretended to be asleep, but watched, wide-eyed, from beneath the covers while Chana stripped down to her underwear before sombrely dressing in long white socks, below-the-knee skirt and a long-sleeved shirt? How she'd lain awake, frightened of being punished, after listening to whispers amongst the cousins – for they had dozens of them – about television, about pop music, and about boyfriends, all of which were *assur*. How could she describe to a stranger about starting school, and of only seeing her brothers at lunchtime, through a wire fence? Of lessons in maths, English and Hebrew, of hours and hours of homework?

"Southgate," Sara said in a sudden rush. "I grew up in Southgate. It was a community house. For the Orthodox community, I mean. Abba was the local Rabbi." Sara paused. All at once she could hear her dad's voice, singing out the Friday night prayers by candlelight. Those nights were magical.

"The front door was always open," she said, smiling as she remembered. "Eema would cook Friday night dinner for whoever wanted to come – lunch on Saturdays, too. Sometimes we'd have fifty people turning up."

Sara could remember the smell of the quiche kept warm on a hot plate overnight, the crispy potato latkes and her mother's homemade maple pecan pie, the thin slices of salt beef that sometimes tasted like they were on the turn. Eema used to pile them into the car to drive 40 minutes to the best value *Glatt Kosher* butchers, where she'd carefully pick out pieces of meat that had been left on the counter, the ends that wouldn't get sold so close to Shabbat. They didn't have much money; never any to spare. Her parents got an allowance from the synagogue, but it was never enough. Yet somehow, they always made do.

Sara told Debbie about watching her brothers set off with their father to walk to *shul*, and the way her mother would go around the house – setting the lights to a timer and unplugging the phone – on Friday afternoons. She told her of the way the girls were expected to help with the housework, while the boys studied from books their sisters weren't allowed to read or touch. "'Weird', they called us," she said of the other kids in the neighbourhood. "And worse." There had been words – terrible words. Symbols, too. Daubed in angry graffiti on the outside of the *shul*; on the wall next to school.

As she talked, what she was describing filled the room. The drab walls newly-painted with scrolls and mezuzahs, the weathered carpets suddenly rich and velvety underfoot, like the red and gold of her parents' faded rug. The light from the modern shade in the ceiling was transformed by flickering, nine-prong strong candlelight; the flowers in the vase on Debbie's windowsill drooping with fruit like the hanging vines of the *sukkah* at *Sukkot*. Simple sounds in the background, of traffic roaring past on Golders Green Road, became the deep intonation of prayers at the *kotel* in Jerusalem, the busy, hawking shouts in the market at the Jaffa Gate, the soul-stirring singing of men joining in with her father – then later, her husband – at every Friday night meal. She told Debbie of leaving her studies in Israel with just a day's notice for London, of being introduced to Avi.

"We went to a café out there," she said, gesturing to the road outside beyond the window. "With a *shadchan*, of course."

"A 'shadchan'?" Debbie repeated.

"A matchmaker, or chaperone," Sara explained. "To help you decide what is important to you in a relationship – your values, the way you wish to bring up your children. I knew then that Avi and I would marry. He had the same wishes as me – to raise a family and to teach them the word of *G-d*."

72

"And what about your feelings for Rebecca, at this time?" Debbie asked.

Sara squirmed in her seat. Hearing her name so casually on somebody else's lips was giving her palpitations. It hurt.

"I... it was impossible," she said. "It's like I told you – like I told Naomi. A Jewish woman must marry and raise a family."

"And you couldn't do that with another woman?" Debbie's eyes strayed to the large plastic clock on the wall as she said it. Their fifty minutes was up.

Sara looked at Debbie and sighed, her reply curdling in her throat. She felt flooded with disappointment. "No," she said flatly. This was the problem. This was her mistake. *Goyim* could never understand.

"Okay, well, we have to wrap things up here but you've done well today, Sara," Debbie said, glancing at the clock again. She stood and motioned to the door. "Why don't you make an appointment for next week with my receptionist? Does the same time suit you?"

Sara pressed her lips together without speaking. She reached down to hook the handle of her handbag around her wrist; swung it upwards onto her lap before standing.

"Thank you," Sara said, walking towards the door. It seemed to have lost its strange power from before she came in, the wood now flat and thin. It was splitting down one of the hinges. As she placed her hand on the brass handle and turned it, Sara knew with some certainty she wouldn't be coming back. What was the point? She had nothing else to say.

"Goodbye," she said, without turning around, then slipped out. She didn't stop at reception, instead walking slowly out of the door and down the narrow flight of stairs that led to the heavy front door. With every step, her chest loosened and she could breathe more easily than before.

Outside on the busy road, traffic blared and people gesticulated out of windows as they attempted to park in small spaces. Lorries unloaded fruit and vegetables to convenience stores, waiters and waitresses loitered in the doorways of restaurants serving either meat, or dairy, or *pareve* food.

Sara slipped out of the doorway of Forest Counselling and adjusted the collar of her shirt. She looked left and right, before quickly stepping down onto the pavement. All around were *frum* women like her, in *sheitels* and scarves, in two-piece suits, three or four or five children hanging from buggies.

Sara smiled and slipped amongst them, knowing she wouldn't stand out. These were her people. She fitted in perfectly.

THE BOAT

I died when I was seven. It was 1980s Apartheid South Africa. I remember the signs for the 'whites-only' beaches and little black kids the same age as me getting hit by policemen carrying truncheons as they begged for ice cream.

We were renting the bottom half of a house owned by a family called Klein, in the foothills of Camps Bay. Table Mountain lurked like a headache in the distance, its halfway cloud creeping in, then out again. There was a miner bird in the garden that used to mimic the sound of the house phone. I loved it when it 'rang', my dad rushing to answer it in case it was work, the dull echo of the ringtone with no one there.

The house was split-level with an annexe on the side, and a maid called Ethel who lived there with her husband. By day her smile was wide and white, her laugh rolling up from somewhere deep within her. At night she would be beaten. The noise was terrible. My mother would stroke my hair and place her hands over my ears to buffet her screams.

The house had a small, turquoise swimming pool at the bottom of the garden, through trees and bushes and eleven steep and winding stone steps. There was a robotic cleaner with a long, black pipe that roamed across the bottom of the pool every evening at six. I darted from corner to corner to avoid it, swimming for my life. I thought of it as an octopus, with one long, terrifying tentacle that would suck me down beneath the surface of the water where I couldn't breathe.

But it wasn't that, that killed me, in the end. It was a cheap, plastic yellow boat with a blow-up giraffe and two

77

holes to put your legs through. Slightly too small for me, slightly too tight. The plastic scratched as I pushed myself in, and scraped as I pulled myself out, leaving raised red welts across my thighs.

The day I died I was on my own at the pool. I'd always been a strong swimmer. My parents didn't need to worry about me, though, as it turned out, they did.

I was surprised, the moment I got trapped in the blow-up boat, upside down. It was too buoyant to flip over again, too strong. I'd always been small for my age, low down on the weight charts. When I was naked you could see my ribs, my heart fluttering in the centre of my chest like a caged bird. My dad had joked about how puffed out he was, how blowing the boat up had tasted of bitter plastic and made his head spin.

I remember fighting as hard as I could. The robot was coming towards me. 'Chug chug chug'. My head under the water. Air leaving my lungs, my throat burning.

As the seconds passed without breathing I twisted my body this way and that, pulling the muscles all the way down one side, growing frantic, but with a kind of detached disbelief. I was seven. My skin was smooth, I had a light spatter of freckles across my nose and cheeks. I'd only just discovered Roald Dahl. This wasn't happening, not to me. I thought that right until the end.

I remember crying out for Dad to save me but my mouth filling with water. It made my teeth hurt, made me cough – only when I drew in to clear it, a rush of cold entered my throat and lungs, filling me up, making me dizzy. It was quiet, beneath the surface of the water. It was like listening from the middle of a dream; space all around me. My eyes and ears foggy, my nose full of wet.

I was too disorientated to know which way was up and for a moment I stayed there, my legs above the surface, static, like I was holding a ballet pose. Then, with my eyes open with the sheer surprise of it all, my hair floating beneath me like a dark and tangled mess of seaweed, I died.

I don't know what happened after that, of course. I imagine that one, maybe both of my parents started to wonder where I was and what I was doing. It would have taken them a while. They were used to me disappearing, sitting in the low branches of a tree, whispering to fairies. They probably imagined me sitting at the bottom of the steps like I liked to do, head on my hands, making up stories.

They most likely called out for me. "Toria," my mum would have said, trilling the 'r', operatic-style, to make me laugh. When I didn't come, she wouldn't have thought anything of it, at first. I'd been diagnosed with glue ear earlier that year, a run of coughs and colds filling my eardrum with fluid. As a consequence, I was almost deaf in my left ear, words and background noise muffled and distant.

After a while she would've turned to my dad. "John," she would have said, exasperated. "Go and see where Victoria's got to, would you." He wouldn't have been listening, caught up with fixing something, paying a bill. She would have had to say it twice, maybe even three times, each time growing more and more annoyed.

Eventually she would have barked for me. Then my dad, walking to some inner beat, jazz on his mind, would have walked out of the large, glass, bifold doors that led to the patio. I can see him standing there, hands on his hips, his bare, strong chest.

He always had such dark hair, my dad. I used to hate it when he asked me to rub suntan lotion on his back, the area between his shoulder blades that he couldn't reach. The bottle of Piz Buin would be sticky, the label peeling away, speckled with sand. The oil would pool across his shoulders, mingle with his sweat. Beneath my tiny hands he was slick and strong. He wasn't a man to me but a mountain, to be climbed, to hang my arms from.

He would've stood there, hands on hips, in his silly yellow swim shorts with the blue lightning bolt flashes. "Toria," he would have shouted in a makeshift Tarzan cry, before stamping down the steps, ape-like. I imagine him clutching his chest when he found me. I don't know if he would have cried. I never saw him cry.

I wonder what he thought when he first saw my legs, waving in the breeze above the surface of the pool, white and still as the sculpture of the bird in Hyde Park. I wonder if, to him, I was beautiful.

FOOD & DRINK

Damascus, 5*

Paradise Circus, Birmingham

There *is* a road to Damascus. For Ali Ahmed, who heads the kitchen at this bustling day-to-night cafe, it is a road littered with flyers for local takeaways, cigarette filters, crisp packets and sorrow.

Ahmed, who trained at the erstwhile *All Seasons Hotel*, fled the violence and brutal warfare in Syria three years ago. In Germany, he worked as a dish-washer; in France, a waiter, before stowing away on a truck that brought him to Britain — and, eventually, to Paradise Circus.

Damascus (named after Ahmed's home city) is hidden in plain sight. It's situated on the first floor above the *Tbilisi Shop* (an Eastern European convenience store), marked by a green sign in Syriac, and is surrounded by industry. The area is undergoing extensive regeneration to make way for hotels and offices. Ahmed flinches every time a drill clatters like gunshot.

"My home in Syria is gone," he tells me, standing in the intimate dining space. "But I have a new home now, here in Birmingham."

Ahmed spent ten years working his way up to become head chef at the *All Seasons* in the Syrian capital, until the hotel was destroyed at the start of the savage conflict in 2011. Twelve years and more than 400,000 deaths later and

83

Damascus has officially opened its doors in the UK. All of the cooks, including Ahmed, have lost loved ones to civil war.

Ahmed's losses include his wife, Yara, and two daughters aged four and seven. His youngest, Haya, had hair like blackberries and a laugh that, Ahmed says, "could make even *Shayṭān* (the devil) smile". Haya was in the care of relatives trying to cross to Europe to join Ahmed in London, when the inflatable dinghy they were in collapsed in the Aegean. Her body was washed up on the shore at Kusadasi, small enough to be mistaken for driftwood.

His eldest daughter – a quiet, studious girl named Sana – was reading beneath a tree in a nearby olive grove when it was bombed and Sana killed. Ahmed keeps the book she was reading, a simple fairytale, under his pillow. Each morning he wakes with ash in his hair.

Everything he does, sees, smells and tastes reminds him of his wife. One night, as the couple were leaving the hotel in Damascus, they were ordered to the ground by three masked men. One of the men began to interrogate him – he thinks with a view to kidnapping him – but a car pulled alongside and began shooting at the men. Yara, also a chef, had spent the day in the kitchens preparing *mahshi*, a famous dish made from vegetables – usually courgette or aubergine – which are stuffed with ground beef, lamb or mutton, nuts and rice. She had been rubbing hand cream into her aching fingers before they left the hotel; before she was shot twice and killed. The scent of rosewater and pink peppercorns rose like a cloud, mixing nauseously with the gunpowder's acrid stink. After that, Ahmed left the country he was born in. He does not know when, or if, he will go back.

When we meet it is Saturday, just past 8am. Ahmed turns minced lamb and pine nuts with a wooden spoon to make *kebab hindi*, while two elderly men sit at a table, measuring out sweet-smelling cinnamon, cloves, allspice, cardamom and nutmeg, ready to season *tabakh rohoo*.

"Heat ghee – then stir in lamb meat – crush together garlic, pinch of salt, dried mint," an octogenarian who calls himself *Jidu* (Syrian for "grandfather") instructs, wielding a pestle and mortar with practiced ease. Jidu fled his home in al-Jinah when the local mosque was levelled in an airstrike, killing 49 worshippers. His wife Safaa is gravely ill and in hospital, and cannot leave. Jidu doesn't always work at Ahmed's cafe; on Sundays he plays the saxophone in busy shopping districts, busking to earn extra cash. He also plays the *oud* (lute), *ney* (flute) and *qanun* (zither), and sings in *maqam*, traditional Arabic music that focuses on melody. *Maqam,* Jidu says, is microtonal, which lends itself to "surges of emotion".

Jidu experiences many surges of emotion while trying to sell the saxophone he has carried around with him since he was a boy. He tapes a handwritten sign carefully to the instrument's weathered black case, which reads: "Saxophone for sale, £300. To save my sick wife." Next to the sign he tacks a faded photograph of his wife taken long ago on their wedding day, her face clear of lines, smile wide and white. He shows us the photo, then wipes his eyes with the back of his hand. He picks up another clove of garlic and crushes it.

Mahmoud, who is somewhere between 60 and 65, waves his fingers in the air, stained red with pomegranate molasses, as he makes *fattoush* – toasted pita salad with tomato and cucumber. "In Syria I was a baker," he explains.

He ran his own business, built his own house, and made his own furniture. Then the house was bombed and he had to leave. He gets out 'before' and 'after' photos from his wallet, of bricks turned to rubble. His tears add a subtle hint of salt to the salad.

Mahmoud says they had 'no choice' but to leave. Following a mass barrel-bombing campaign by the Syrian regime in 2013, his wife's brother, a veterinarian, began posting anti-Assad comments on his Facebook page. The Air Force Intelligence Unit came to find him. He was tortured and killed.

The menu is simple at *Damascus*. All dishes are paragons of traditional Syrian fare, and Ahmed says he got most of the recipes from his father, who was also a chef. He died, aged seventy-five, in US-led air strikes launched by international coalition forces, following US President Donald Trump's campaign trail pledge to "bomb the s**t out of Isis". Ahmed found him on the ground clutching a photograph of his mother, who had died the year before in a massacre in Aleppo. Ahmed was close enough to feel his breath against his cheek; to hear him whisper, "I love you, son," through parched lips. He turned away, desperately, to find water. When he returned, he was gone.

He remembers his father, Hassan Ahmed, as a man who 'rarely smiled'. He was stern, but — Ahmed insists — he had to be. "He was a teacher, but teachers earn very little in Syria," he says. "And so he also ran a mobile phone shop." As bombs turned the city to ruins and swallowed up schools, money became tight. Ahmed's father was forced to sell his wife's jewellery. Ironically, he says, Ahmed's father was a 'great fan' of President Bashar al-Assad, the British-trained ophthalmologist who became leader of Syria seventeen years ago, inheriting the position from his father, Hafez al-Assad. "He loved Bashar." As his country began to disappear, his father maintained the man he so admired could not be responsible for so much bloodshed. "A doctor would not do this," he told his son. Still, when the suffering became too great he went to Aleppo to try to borrow money from 'bad men' to pay smugglers to take his family across the sea to Europe. But he never saw water again.

Besides *tabbouleh* and *fattoush*, there is *moutabal* (smokey aubergines swathed with yoghurt) and *falafel*, which Ahmed serves with homemade tahini and pickles from a nearby Lebanese-run shop. Sometimes people on the street call him names, like 'Paki'. When he says he has never been to Pakistan, that he is, in fact, from Syria; they call him 'refugee scum' and tell him to 'fuck off back where he came from'. Ahmed, who is nevertheless 'excited' to share his country's traditional food with Birmingham locals, says living in Britain 'sometimes feels dangerous, sometimes scary, sometimes good'. He does not blame some people for disliking refugees. "They don't know anything about refugees, they just hear about us on the news."

While we are talking, Ahmed chops meat on a butchers' slab. His fingers come away bloody, and he stumbles, wipes sweat from his brow, rubs his short black moustache with his fingers. He apologises. He says today he is not feeling himself, that he feels sad because Amir, the fifteen-year-old nephew of a friend of his, recently suffered a fractured spine and a brain haemorrhage after having an 'encounter' at a local shopping centre. Amir had been studying English at college and liked playing dominoes. Twenty people have been arrested. None have been charged.

Rotating daily specials include Syrian meatball stew (*kebab hindi*), spiced chicken with cardamom and rice (*kabsa*) and vegetable and tamarind stew (*tabakh rohoo*) that Ahmed likens to 'British casserole'. For dessert, an assortment of rich, sweet, packages of pastry made of layers of filo filled with chopped nuts and sweetened with honey (*baklava*), served with cardamom tea. Ahmed's sister, Berna, was famed throughout Damascus for the moist texture and delicate taste of her *baklava*. Berna (from the Turkish, meaning 'strong and brave as a bear') was kidnapped by Isis fighters on a trip to the *souq* (market) in 2015 and taken to Raqqa. Ahmed cries a little when he talks about her. He does not know if she is still alive.

"It is very bad in Raqqa," he says. "There are public hangings, killings. If someone steals something because they are hungry, Isis puts their hands in boiling oil."

Ahmed says he receives calls from people trapped in the region who report horrors such as women being flogged in the street for showing their hands, young boys thrown from the top of tall buildings for being gay. He mentions a friend whose twelve-year-old daughter was forced to marry an Isis fighter; while her son, thirteen, was beaten and taken to a police station for wearing jeans. Ahmed asks to go outside to catch his breath. When he returns, his apron is streaked with moisture. He remembers the exact colour of Berna's eyes, "like the sea after a storm settles".

We take a moment to sit at one of the small tables, lit by a hand-beaded lamp. The décor borders on the bedouin: diners sit on sofas scattered with multi-coloured rugs. "I want it to be cosy and for people to feel like they are at home," Ahmed says of the aesthetic. His voice is gruff and he coughs several times to clear his throat. He admits he is tired. The low-level lighting disguises the rips in the seat-coverings; the walls, smeared with cracks.

On the wall in the kitchen, next to photographs of his wife, his daughters and his parents, there is a snapshot of another young woman, cradling a baby. "My other sister, Amena," Ahmed says, leaning on the edge of the metal sink. "She is holding my nephew." He says she paid traffickers to travel from Syria to Italy with her son, Zain, when he was just ten months old. They hunkered down in the crowded hold of a boat alongside 800 others. The water was rough and choppy. There were no toilets. The smugglers threw occasional tins of food down the hatch. "Zain was breastfeeding," Ahmed says, his lips tight and white at the edges. "But after the journey he stopped eating."

Amena smuggled the baby to France for medical treatment, but while she was there she was assaulted in the street by a man who kicked her to the floor and tried to pull off her *hijab* (headscarf). She was afraid, so she hid in a lorry carrying frozen goods to Britain. Zain died before she reached the border. She is now living in York while she waits for her asylum claim to be processed. She is not allowed to work and lives on just £35 a week. She has been forced to beg. Sometimes, Ahmed says, strangers say terrible things. Sometimes, they spit on her, or worse. Ahmed slaps the pieces of meat he has chopped on a board covered in flour, seasons it with salt and pepper.

Later, Ahmed layers parcels of food carefully in white linen – spinach and feta *fatayer* (pie), *ka'ach bilmalch* (sesame biscuits with salt), *kofta* (lamb meatballs) and Syrian grape leaves stuffed with a lemony and garlicky rice filling. Wrapped up, they resemble burial shrouds.

"It is for the homeless," he explains, pointing at the street outside. "People are hungry. I am a chef. I can feed them." The future for *Damascus* is unknown. Ahmed only has a licence to sell food until March. After that, he does not know if he will be able to pay the rent for his small bedsit apartment above a neighbouring McDonald's. His application for asylum is pending. (*Dishes, £4 - £9*).

BELOW THE LINE

The first comment comes with a self-righteous whiff of semen. "Who is this 'woman'?", in intermittent and indignant Caps Lock. "Who IS she?"

I sit beneath the window, bottle of beer in hand, pondering my enforced existential crisis. It is almost nine in the evening. I left work hours ago. I only turned my laptop on out of an egotistical desire to see how many 'shares' I'd had. And I knew, of course I knew what I would find when I got there. You don't write a column about sexism without attracting the attention of pigs.

My index finger caresses the circular wheel of the mouse like a clit, scrolling, scrolling. Ninety-six comments. I raise an eyebrow, take a swig of warm lager. I know I shouldn't, but I can't help myself. And I'm amused, at least at first. *Who AM I?* I've wondered that myself, half cut on a bottle of wine, gazing out at the street with the lights off. I like to watch them out there, courting, weaving, fighting, fucking. A voyeur to savagery.

"Silly slut," they froth as I read on, sounding strangely Victorian. "Whore," they self-congratulate. "Stupid bitch," they spit. And then they get personal. "I would," one says, like he's being complimentary. "You blind?" another counters. "You'd have to wear beer goggles to fuck *that*."

I imagine them sitting at home in identikit fury behind the smooth, safe glass of their computer monitors, keyboard warriors, anti-heroes, trolls. They are united in their desire to slash me, inch by column inch, dissect my margins, decapitate my byline.

"Ugly", they spew, "evil", a "sanctimonious hypocrite". A "self-serving, middle-class princess making a power grab by bullying women and demonising men," part of an "utterly loathsome creed." I sit back, stung. Despite myself, despite everything, "ugly" wounds me.

"She obviously can't get a bloke," types Steve_365. "Someone should rape her, teach her a lesson." I shut down the screen without turning the power off.

Later that evening, my dad calls. "I'm worried you're getting a reputation," he says. "As a bit of a… 'feminist'." This, he whispers.

I roll my eyes, make platitudes. Before I go to bed, I tap out a message to Steve_365. "Thanks for the feedback," I reply, evenly. "Can we meet to discuss? I'm writing an article on trolling."

I turn and bury my face into the coldness of the pillow. Perhaps I've only got myself to blame. Everyone says never read the comments.

A week passes, then I'm sitting in a trendy café on a building site in Hackney, waiting for Steve_365. It is five in the afternoon and close to closing. The waitress has gone out the back to smoke a fag. I am jumpy, keep my hand on my phone. I'm ninety per cent sure Steve_365's rape threats were just that – threats – but you can't be too careful.

The door creaks and a pale, overweight man in his mid-thirties comes in. He's wearing a red football shirt. He doesn't meet my eyes.

"Steve?" I stand, think about putting my hand out to shake his, then retract it and wipe it on my jeans instead.

"It's Phil, actually," he mumbles, staring at the dirty lino. He scrapes a chair along the floor and sits down warily, a metre or so from me. There's a brown stain beneath his collar. I sit back down.

"Thanks for coming," I say. "I think it's really brave, actually," I add, fishing around in my bag.

"What is?" Steve, or Phil, pipes up. He lights a cigarette, despite the ban, leaving it to hang limply from the corner of his mouth, ash wrinkled to the tip like foreskin.

"You," I say, bringing my hand to my lap. "Agreeing to meet me like this. After the things you said."

Phil's doughy cheeks redden. "Look, that was just a joke, okay?"

I shrug. "Okay."

He looks uncertain.

"It doesn't matter," I continue, "you'll still be able to help me – with my article, I mean."

I take out the knife and place it on the table between us. It lies there, gloriously erect, a full 12 inches of steel.

"As I said," I continue, "I'm writing about castration. I'm so glad you could contribute."

ELEPHANTS DON'T LIVE IN THE JUNGLE

At two in the morning, an alarm goes off.

I hear it echoing at the nurses' station, a reverberating beep from the machine attached to the bed opposite that spreads across the ward like disease. It sounds different to the usual hospital cacophony of bleeps and hoots. It is louder, more frantic. It is followed by the squeak of two or three pairs of feet, pounding against lime-green linoleum, then the metal trill of a curtain being thrust aside.

Someone is wailing. English mixed with... Polish, Ukrainian, perhaps. "What to do?" the voice cries, husky with tears. "Do something. Please. What to do?"

I hear Jackie, one of the nurses. She peeked into our cubicle last night, stout and cheerful, to warn us she was going to turn the lights off. "Time for bed, mummy! She's on two-hourly obs. Get some rest."

Now, Jackie's voice comes from a distance, coated in solace. "We're doing everything we can." I picture her soft face grown serious, her small eyes squinting from behind thick, black frames.

I lie on my side on a camp bed, bruised hip against starched sheets, trying to tune out whatever is taking place just metres away. Ellie is sleeping on a raised cot to my right, her blonde hair matted to her forehead with sweat, her cheeks aflame. I look past her and fixate on the amber numbers flashing against a black screen, her heart in digits. Each time it rises above 150, our machine bleats its own warning, like a ship lost in fog.

A sharp smell of shit wafts across the room, accompanied by more crying. "Look at him," she is saying. "Look at him. Please. He is not usually like this."

"Mummy, I understand how you feel, but we're doing all the tests we can. We don't know what's wrong because he can't tell us. What do you want us to do?"

I bristle on her behalf. Do the nurses refer to all relatives as 'mummy' like this, I wonder – rather than by name? It is easier for them, I expect, than reading notes, but it sounds pejorative, reduces us to invisible, anxious, nameless entities, pacing beside rows of identical beds. Together we are simply 'parents', an amorphous mass of angst and guilt, fear and gallows humour.

I raise an eyebrow sarcastically – knowingly – though there's nobody to see it. The mattress is stiff beneath my back. I flex the muscles in my buttocks until they tremble and stare straight ahead at the blue curtain. There is a red 'no entry' sign at the corner. "Respect my privacy!" it orders. "Please ask before entering!" I gaze beyond it, willing it to open, torn between wanting to see the 'mummy' beyond, with her stricken charge, and wanting to stay hidden.

Ellie's heart monitor taunts me with a sudden succession of increasingly noisy bleeps. I glance over at it, 172. Something thick and viscous rises in my throat. 189. I hear sirens calling from the deep. The numbers flash up to 207, and I'm drowning. I'm half out of the bed. I don't know what to do with my hands.

The numbers stutter for one second – two – and then begin to fall again, settling at 180. I sit back down, concentrate on breathing. Nobody comes and I consider walking to the other side of the room to turn off the alarm, but I feel stuck to the bed, weighted there. There are no flowers on our bedside table and I wonder if that's a rule or if I've been remiss, somehow, in forgetting to bring some.

"With normal children, we can see where the pain is coming from." Jackie's voice floats across the ward, muffled and indistinct. She must be bending over the boy. "With your son it's more difficult."

"He's only ten – what kind of life is this?" his mother cries. I hear sniffs and choking sounds, the rustle of a tissue.

"Is there anyone who can support you? Take over to give you a break?" This is a new voice, a soft, caramelly voice. The mother doesn't answer.

I put my fingers in my ears and lie back down, close my eyes. My mind is racing. I can't hold on to my thoughts. As soon as I try to focus on something it scatters, like rings of smoke evaporating outside a pub on a cold night. Cigarettes and carefree camaraderie. It feels like forever since we were out without Ellie, out without worrying about her breathing and whether or not whoever was looking after her would recognise the signs, would know when to give her the blue pump, would understand when it wasn't working; when to call an ambulance. I push images of blue flashing lights away, think instead of the house, wonder if my husband has remembered to feed the cat, hope he's not fretting alone in our bed. He can't sleep here with us, for our small section of the ward is cramped and impossible. A cot, a camp bed, a chair next to the sink. If he stayed he would have to lean his head against the taps, as if he were having his hair washed at a salon. Those salon sinks are never comfortable. Why not?

Surely they could have come up with something better by now than a rolled-up towel around your neck to stop you getting whiplash? The head massages are good, though. Worth a tip alone. If Ellie gets better soon – when she gets better soon, I correct myself – I'll treat us to a mother-daughter trip to the hairdressers. They always give her a free lollipop before we leave. She loves that.

I open my eyes and study the ceiling, crack every knuckle methodically from thumb to little finger on both hands. I do it though I know I shouldn't, it might give me arthritis, though that's probably an old wives' tale. Arthritis would stop me from renovating the house, would stop me stripping paint, wallpapering the ceiling. And then where would we be? I think about the woodworm we need to get treated in the cellar, wonder who I should call to sort it out, feel a flutter in my chest when I contemplate the work involved – how hard it will be to lift the carpets and floorboards and how much it'll all cost. I massage my temples and place the palm of my hand over my eyes and forehead. It feels hot to the touch, slightly clammy. Something hurts and I grope beneath my clothes, feel the angry gland in my armpit. The room is suffocating.

The boy opposite suddenly cries out, interrupting my thoughts. He is awake, probably terrified, unsure where he is or what he is doing. "Hawwww," he honks loudly, like a barking seal. "Hawwww." His mother clucks at him from between her teeth, like she's calming a housecat. I can no longer hear the nurses and imagine they've slipped away, helpless in their soft-soled slippers, pretending they can't hear him – or her.

The metal rings at the edge of the curtain pole clash unexpectedly against each other, making me jump, as someone comes into our cubicle from the side. He is tall and kind-faced. I give him a rictus grin of welcome and glance at my phone. It is three in the morning.

"I am Percival," he says softly. He speaks softly, his words coated in honey. "I am one of the nurses looking after you tonight."

I prop myself up on my elbow and watch him move towards the monitor. The light from the lamp behind the head of the cot renders him a tall, wiry silhouette. Ellie's chest rises and falls rapidly as she sleeps. He reaches for the probe attached to her toe. It is stuck to her skin with rough beige tape. He presses down gently on the red light and the smaller numbers on the monitor to the left of those measuring her heart – her oxygen levels – falter and then rise, almost imperceptibly. 92 per cent or more and you can go home, they said when we first arrived for assessment in A&E. Ellie is on 88 per cent.

"We need to give her some oxygen," Percival says, pressing something on the monitor to stop the bleeping. The silence is scant relief. He reaches for a plastic mask, bound by green elastic.

I reach out to stop him. "Do we have to put it over her face?"

He turns to look at me while reaching with his right hand for the valve marked O2. "You don't want to put it over her face?"

I shake my head. "It might wake her," I whisper. "She'll be scared."

101

He nods and turns the valve clockwise, still holding the mask. A faint hiss of gas comes from the mouth and nose-shaped plastic. He turns the dial further and the hiss gets louder. I glance at Ellie, worried it will wake her up. She stirs but stays asleep, the reddish-purple of her lips pressing together as she grinds her teeth.

That's how I first noticed something was wrong, when the soft pink of her mouth took on a blueish tinge. Then I saw the tell-tale dip at the base of her throat, the way her ribs were drawing in, sharp as knives, with every breath. In a terrifyingly short space of time the gaps between those breaths got shorter and shorter until she was gasping for air.

Percival slowly brings the mask down to rest on Ellie's pillow, centimetres from her face. He fusses with it, makes sure it has a clear path. We both turn our attention to the monitor. I only realise I have been holding my breath when the numbers on the left start to rise. 89 per cent… 92 per cent. They come to rest at 95 per cent and I exhale and smile, for real this time, for what feels like the first time. "Thank you," I say, feeling my chapped lips with my tongue.

"Ah, you're welcome," Percival says, in the soft lilt of sandy beaches and palm trees. "Why don't you go and get yourself some tea? She'll be sleeping a while, now. The oxygen will help her."

I nod and sit up, rub my aching thighs, wipe gritty sleep from the corners of my eyes with my fingers. I yawn and haul my legs out from beneath the thin green blanket to the floor. It is sticky against my toes. I push myself off the low bed and stretch out my spine like a cat. It makes a series of satisfying pops. Then I grasp the corner of the blue curtain and step out onto the main ward.

The curtain opposite is open a metre or so, and I can't help myself from glancing in. The mother lies on the camp bed, a light green hospital blanket wrapped tightly around her, eyes closed. She is wearing jeans and odd socks – one striped, the other spotted. She looks exhausted. Her son is in the cot, his body bent at impossible proportions, clenched in sleep. He coos as I walk past, gnarled fingers grasping at the corner of his pillow. A faint silver line of spittle stretches from the corner of his mouth. I walk away as quickly as I can, as though their illness might be catching. As I go, I send up silent thanks to a God I don't believe in that he isn't my child. "Take him, not her," I ask without making a sound, guilt causing me to look behind me, in case I am caught. I feel sick with shame.

In the parents' room, I can breathe again. I shake off the feelings of suffocation. Dull as it is in this grey room, cold and bleak as it is, the double doors nevertheless remove it from the night-time moans and cries of the children's ward. I walk to where the kettle sits on a smeared work surface in a small and poky kitchen. The kettle is hot to the touch. Someone must have been here just moments ago, mixing their own sorrow into a warm drink. I take out the shared milk from the fridge below the sink and a teabag from a large plastic container. I add both to a polystyrene cup, the sound of my nails scratching against it setting my teeth on edge. I pour over the water, add two sachets of sugar and give it a lacklustre stir with a plastic spoon. I walk into the main part of the room and sit on a pinched, dark red leather sofa, sweet tea hot between my fingers.

I take a loud sip. The steam stings my eyes. The walls around me are devoid of decoration, save for a blue noticeboard above my head. I turn to study the leaflets pinned to it. It makes for grim reading. Support groups for pregnant women and children who have experienced FGM. A badly-laminated warning: 'No hot drinks on the ward.' A teenager's face staring out from behind stark lettering: 'He says he won't take care of me anymore unless I have sex with his friends,' and beneath it, in red: 'Stop child sex exploitation NOW.' A photocopied Christmas charity appeal to provide toys for the playroom. I make a mental note to contribute, and wonder if it matters that it's January. I take a few loud, slurping sips of my tea. It warms me slowly from the inside.

I've only been sitting a few moments when a cleaner disturbs my solitude, clattering in with a mop, bucket and plastic bag to change the bins. I realise I have no idea what time it is. I finish the last of my tea, suddenly worried that Ellie may have woken up, alone and afraid, that her oxygen levels may have plummeted. A rising wave of panic begins in my chest and spreads out to my fingers. I throw my cup away and stride out of the room, my heart thundering in my ears. I turn right out of the double doors, past the stand marked 'aquarium' that's missing an aquarium, the closed playroom door and a private room bearing a red warning sign. 'Infection control', it reads. Inside, a tiny baby sleeps alone in a small cot with high blue metal bars. Where are its parents?

I break into a run halfway back to bed fifteen. The curtain masking the boy opposite has been closed. I am grateful, and guilt-ridden for feeling grateful. I push the corner of the curtain open to our beds. She's still asleep. I lean over her, study the soft, upturned curve of her nose, brush away a soft curl stuck to her forehead. I stroke her cheek, careful not to wake her.

I plop down on the chair next to the bed to watch the monitor. I've only had a few hours of sleep but I feel wired. Time passes in a vacuum, here. I haven't opened my book, haven't checked my phone for Twitter or Facebook. I don't know what I've been doing, yet hours have passed, somehow. I've been here with her two nights already.

In the morning her dad will visit, pass through before he has to decide whether to go to work. If she's no better, he'll call in sick, then stay with us, before going home to rest, like he did last night. A brief flash of heat – of anger – ripples through me. I wonder if he realises how little sleep I'm getting amidst the constant bleeps and whistles. I imagine when he comes in the morning he'll look unshaven and beaten up with worry, as if he's the one who has stayed up all night. If he mentions how tired he is, I think, I'll murder him. Though of course, it's not like I could do anything else. Ellie needs me. And I need her.

At dinner recently a friend asked me casually whether she was a 'mummy's girl' or a 'daddy's girl'. I paused, a forkful of tapas halfway to my mouth, to think about it. But I couldn't really answer. When she's sick or hurts herself, Ellie reaches out for me to soothe her. But in the middle of the night, after a bad dream, or when she's looking for a playmate, it's "Daddy! Dad....dy!" we hear echoing through the narrow space between our bedrooms.

'Daddy'. 'Mummy'. When did we start calling each other that? I can't remember life before Ellie, though it was a mere four years ago. We used to have time for ourselves, for each other. I bought and wore pretty clothes, had my nails done with friends at weekends. I look at them now. They are rough and uneven, the teal polish I put on weeks ago at Ellie's insistence peeling in the centres like a Rorschach painting. I pick at a loose thread of skin but I scratch too far and I bleed. I put it in my mouth and suck it until I can't feel it anymore.

A new sound starts up beyond the curtain to my left, a deep, tonal hum that grows and grows before reaching climax. At its own private apogee it stutters before starting all over again, building to a new crescendo. I cock my head to the side to listen. It sounds like drilling, or vacuuming. I close my eyes, trying to place it. It's coming from the space next to me. I know a Bangladeshi family are there, a mother and a six-year-old girl. The girl seems to have a similar condition to Ellie, an asthma that, according to what I've overheard, keeps her on the ward for two weeks at a time – even over Christmas. I've heard her cry with rapid, rattling gasps as she struggles for air. The mother has a six-month-old baby she's left at home with an aunt. She's been struggling to explain in broken English to the nurses that she needs to breastfeed, but they won't let her bring the baby onto the ward in case he picks up any germs. Instead, they've given her a pump. And then clicks. This is the sound I'm hearing – the low, ignoble drone of a breast pump that sucks liquid gold like it's siphoning milk from the udders of a cow.

I yawn, feeling a hot, prickling sensation at the corners of my eyes. My body is dull and heavy. I need sleep. I am sick with need for it. The camp bed next to Ellie looks lonely and I crawl up onto her raised bed and press myself into her curved, flushed warmth. I lay one arm over and across her stomach. She's so tiny I could scoop her up entirely in the crook of my elbow. I kiss her forehead and tuck my other arm

106

under the edge of her pillow. I nudge the oxygen mask closer to her face with my nose and close my eyes.

I shoot awake, adrenaline shooting through my body, my heart pounding like I've just run a 10k race. I did that once, for charity. I'd done no training and my legs ached for days. I turn my head slowly from left to right, my neck sore. It is bright on the ward, curtains open, daytime officially declared. I can hear kids playing and laughing in the small playground outside. I look to my left to find Ellie still dead to the world, the soft rise and fall of her chest comforting me a little. Her stats aren't much better, but they're no worse, at least. I shift uncomfortably on the bed. I need to go to the toilet.

I get down gingerly, shaking the sting of pins and needles away. I slip out onto the ward and glance at the bed opposite – I expect their curtain to be closed, anticipate hearing the steady bleeps of the machines, the wails of the boy, the stifled sobs of the mother. But the bed is in view, freshly made, a white pillow tucked neatly beneath a thin, green blanket. There are no creases on the bedsheets. There's no sign they've been there at all.

I approach the nurses' station and pause, unsure of what I am going to say until I say it. A nurse I don't recognise is sitting behind the cluttered desk, absorbed in paperwork. "Um, excuse me," I venture, clearing my throat. My voice is rough and a little wobbly. She looks up expectantly.

"What do you need, mummy?"

I gesture back towards our corner of the ward. "I was just wondering what happened... to the boy opposite, I mean. And his mother. I think they were Polish, or something like that... Did they leave? Is he okay? Is she okay? I mean, I don't expect you can tell me..."

The nurse smiles but it doesn't meet her eyes. "I'm sorry," she says. She looks back at her notes. I stand there lamely for a moment, wondering what to do next. I look again, but the empty bed makes me shiver.

I decide to stretch my legs, walking in the opposite direction to the Parents' Room. I duck into a toilet, relieve myself and splash water on my face and neck. There is a shower in the corner of the bathroom. I long to turn it on until it is scalding, imagine standing beneath it with my eyes closed, streams of hot water running down my chin and breasts. I'll ask the nurses for a towel when I get a chance, I think dully. In the mirror, my skin is sallow. I scratch at a blackhead that's appeared on my chin, try to smooth out the fine lines between my eyebrows. Small clumps of sticky black mascara are stuck to the ends of my lashes. I can't remember when I put it on. I place a hand on my stomach, feel its small curve pressing against my vest top. The skin there is soft and stretched. It still bears the jagged silver marks of Ellie's birth. I dry my hands on a scratchy paper towel and exit the bathroom, turning left, further from the ward. Ahead is a door marked 'School Room'. There's some kind of clanging noise emanating from within, and when I get closer I see it is full of people holding instruments.

"Oh, do come in, mummy!" A woman throws open the door and rushes towards me. She is wearing a purple scarf around her head and long feather earrings. She's at it too with the 'mummy' talk, I think, raising an eyebrow. She beams at me, oblivious.

"I'm Serena," she says, in a bubbly, breathy voice. She gestures around the table, introducing three other adults, whose names I instantly forget. One holds a violin, one a trumpet, another a clarinet. There are children around the table, too; our six-year-old neighbour with asthma and two boys, around twelve and fourteen. They're in hospital gowns. The adults must be their parents. Serena hands the younger ones bells on sticks to ring, and the oldest boy a cymbal. To the adults – including me – she gives maracas.

"We're going to make the sound of the rainforest!" She is giddy with glee. "And Malachi, as soon as we get to the height of the storm, you're going to bang the cymbal together, like this!" Serena turns to the fourteen-year-old, who looks like he wants to die of embarrassment, and claps her hands together in an exaggerated clash. He responds by pulling his beanie down over his eyes and shaking his head in silent, self-conscious prayer.

"Now, before we begin, we must have a story! What's our story?" Serena skips to the front of the room and puts pen to whiteboard. She looks around the room expectantly. "Remember – this room is the rainforest!" She pronounces 'rainforest' with a trill on the 'r', bringing her fingers up and waggling them in front of her face. "Let's have an animal. What's your favourite animal?" As she says this, she bends low and beams directly into the face of the six-year-old, who shrinks into her chair.

"A fly," she whispers.

Serena hesitates for a fraction of a second. "A fly!" she repeats. "Now isn't that unusual!" Serena beams and writes FLY in curly, capital letters on the board. She turns around and adopts a thoughtful pose, the thumb and index fingers of her left hand tapping her chin. "Hmmmm," she buzzes loudly. "I'm thinking flies and elephants go together well, so... yes!" At this, she claps her hands. "That's an *excellent* idea! Let's have an elephant, as well! Where do elephants live?" This time, she doesn't even pause for a response – and she doesn't get one. I sneak a glance at the other adults in the room. They are staring at her, slack-jawed and open-mouthed. Serena has finished writing the word 'jungle' and is embarking on a picture of a smiling monkey next to it when Malachi pipes up.

"The savanna," he grunts.

"What's that, Malachi?" Serena trills, turning around slowly. She holds her pen aloft, and behind her smile, she looks a little wary. "I didn't hear you!"

"Elephants. They live in the savanna. Not the jungle."

"Oh!" She smiles, eyes searching the ceiling. "Right. That's right. But this is our story, and in our story, elephants live in the jungle, don't they!"

"No, they don't."

Serena's smile is fading. "Well, I don't think we need to be literal, Malachi! Come on! We're having fun!"

"I'm a very literal person," he mutters. I look at him and stifle a smile. I'm starting to like Malachi.

Serena, evidently, feels differently. I can't help but admire her, for she doesn't even falter. She simply ignores him. "O...kay. Now. Who can tell me what elephants like to eat?"

"Bananas?" This, from the 12-year-old.

"Thank you, Gene! Someone is being positive and we like positivity in the school room, don't we?"

She writes 'bananas' on the board. "And what do we think happens to the elephants after they eat the bananas? Do they lie down for a nice sleep?"

"They get food poisoning," Malachi says dryly. I can't help myself – I snort and try to disguise it as a cough. I turn to make a funny face at Ellie, then realise she's not there. I rise from my chair in a panic, remember where she is; where I am. I need to get back to her before she wakes up. But I am torn. I know consciously that she will be okay – that the nurses are just metres away from her cot, that Percival will be checking on her. I want to see this out, in this room, right here. It'll make a fantastic story to entertain Ellie with, to tell Mike, to recount to family and friends once we're out of hospital and the horror is over, I reason. I make a bargain with myself. If I stay another five minutes, Ellie will just be waking up when I get back. If I stay, she'll be okay. Nothing bad can happen in this bizarre and surreal room of elephants, food poisoning and music. I can't leave until this is over. Serena's rainforest will be my talisman.

But Serena isn't sure what to do. She stands, chewing the end of the whiteboard marker, before hesitantly writing down the words, 'elly belly'. "There," she says, chewing her lip. "We've talked about elephants and flies, and now they've got tummy trouble." One of the parents at the back gives a loud snort.

"Do you know what?" Serena turns, gurning strangely, and puts the pen down. "I think it's time to forget the story and make some music!" She rushes to the table and takes a seat, picking up a small electronic keyboard. "Right, everyone. Let's start by tapping our fingers, gently, wherever you want to make a noise. On the table, on your instruments, just tap

111

and pluck away. And... go!"

Serena is getting excited. She gestures at us to raise the volume, and I ring the bell, louder than before. Malachi is tapping a triangle at half the speed of everyone else. It is just off.

"Now mummies — daddies — shake those maracas! That's it!" Serena raises her hands high over her head to spur us on. The ringing and shaking obediently grows louder and louder, and I worry briefly about the other kids on the ward, the ones who are too weary or too sick to join in. I think of Ellie and glance towards the door. I really must get back to her. *"Just two more minutes here and she'll be okay,"* I think desperately. *"Everything will be okay."* Serena jiggles in her seat, her hands waggling frantically above her head, like she's a medium leading a séance.

We shake, rattle, ring, buzz and hum, and my arm begins to ache. The other parents are grinning maniacally, and I wonder whether they're really enjoying themselves or whether they've been caught up in the strange collective madness of the moment. The trumpet parps, the clarinet whistles, bells chime and even Malachi has his eyes closed as the triangle 'dings' wildly. We are reaching some kind of crescendo, and with it, I feel both elated and a little afraid. I want it to end, can feel the tightness in my chest at the thought of having left Ellie alone so long, mixed with the bizarre sense of not wanting to let Serena down. I want to run head long out of the door and back to our cubicle, yet a part of me is reluctant to return to the sadness of the ward.

Just then, Serena pulls a sharp conductor's pause in the air, and we stop, panting and looking around at each other. The room feels charged, somehow – like we've shared something, though none of us knows quite what it is. The silence stretches for one beat, two. Someone clears their throat. We all turn as one to stare at Malachi, tension like a live cable in the centre of the room, crackling and sparking. Serena nods at him to make the final clash on the cymbal, her eyes wide and encouraging, almost pleading, and I stare at him and realise I am pleading too, looking down at the instrument which lies placidly on his lap. If he does this... I think, Ellie will get better. The boy from the curtain opposite will make a miraculous recovery. His mother will stop crying. All these sick children, they'll be healed. It is ridiculous. It is naïve. It is hope. I recognise it and I cling to it, with every fibre of my being.

We stare at the cymbal, the unmoving thing, transfixed. The clock ticks. We wait.

THINGS MY MOTHER NEVER TOLD ME

When I turned five, my mother sat me down, handed me a prosthetic leg and told me I would marry the person who fit in it. I looked at it and frowned. It wasn't the Cinderella story I'd seen on TV. That was a glass slipper, not a plastic foot. I didn't know where this horrible old leg had come from, or why we had it. Besides, nobody in my family was without one; at least, not that I knew. It was a funny pink colour and came up to my waist. It felt hollow and when I rapped on it my knuckles made a *plink plink plink* noise, like the woodpecker that knocked every night on the old oak in the back garden, slurping up bugs and sticky sap. What if there were worms inside the leg? What if they burrowed out of the hole at the top in the night and slimed all over my bed, all over my stomach or worse? I didn't understand. I pushed the leg away and told her I didn't want it, that I was scared. She took it from me and put it away somewhere and didn't say a word.

When she presented me with the leg again, it was my tenth birthday and I was achingly disappointed. She'd wrapped it up in paper with glitter stars and a bright bow, and I'd thought it was a tennis racket. When I pulled the leg out, instead; I cried with disappointment. It wasn't bright green and laser-cut, like Jerome's 3D-printed hand. His gleamed incandescent every time he raised it in class to answer a question about the planets; about Jupiter, the biggest of them all, the gas giant with the white spot on its surface like a sightless eye, the secret storm that's been raging for hundreds of years in dark space. His hand had silver lightning flashes running down the knuckles and pointed fingers like Wolverine. His hand was *cool*. "It doesn't even have sensors or adjustable sockets," I whined, sticking my tongue out. My mother sighed and shook her head, muttered something about me being spoilt. She took it from me and put it back in the loft.

She started mentioning it, occasionally, over dinner, even when it was nowhere near my birthday. Our 'legacy', she called it; like it was all some big joke. She likened it to a family heirloom – like a locket, or beautiful pendant – but I was thirteen; and my best friends Ali and Constance had come over for pizza. They were blonde and shiny-haired and giggled behind their hands and gave each other knowing looks. They must've told people at school, because people started saying Mum was 'mad' and that she'd 'lost it' and 'no wonder, after what her dad did to her'. My cheeks burned with bright red shame and I threatened to deck anyone who spoke about Mum like that again. And anyway, Dad hadn't done a thing. He was a war hero. He'd been blown to bits saving a bus-load of children in Afghanistan, that's what Mum said. They'd patched him back together and gave him a prosthetic arm to match the prosthetic leg. He'd come home, all haunted by what he'd seen in the war, and drank too much and ended up falling under a train. It wasn't his fault. They'd sent the leg back to us, because that was all that was left of him. That's where it had come from. Mum had told me now I was old enough 'to understand'. I didn't remember him, apart from in photos.

By fifteen I'd started walking out of the room whenever Mum started on about Dad, and how much she missed him, and how it wasn't his fault that he got so angry, and that all heroes have their dark sides. Apparently Dad had saved an entire congregation of church-goers from being shot to death by the Taliban, but ended up getting shot himself; and when I said I thought it was a bus-load of school children that he'd saved, she went all quiet and said I must be 'confused'. I didn't like thinking about Dad, and anyway, I couldn't sleep for thinking about Lisa. She was captain of the netball team and had long, smooth arms that were tanned and perfectly hairless. She played *Goal Attack* to my *Goal Defence*. I found myself making stupid jokes around her and kicking myself for it afterwards. We kissed while putting the bibs away in the small hut at the back of the netball court, on a late afternoon in January, the sky dark pink above our heads. It was cold. There were countless stars. The kiss hung in the air like an ice sculpture, so fragile I knew it would shatter. And it did. I plucked frozen shards from my lips every night for thirty-six nights, worn down to slush by morning. After our last match of the season, my mum brought down the old leather bag from the loft and opened it to reveal the leg lying there, immobile, on a bed of black velvet, like a tiny corpse in a coffin. She stroked it lovingly and told me I needed to find 'true love', like she had, before she'd 'messed it up' by not being quite perfect.

"Fuck off," I said, wrinkling my nose, my heart thumping like gunshot. "I don't want that fucking thing anywhere near me." She sobbed all night and I scratched myself until I bled because I felt so bad about it.

At seventeen, I finally moved out. I'd had to start wearing ear-plugs to drown out the sounds of Mum sobbing all night; started spending time drifting around carparks and bars at night until two or three so I didn't have to watch her stroking and kissing that leg. The doctor had given her pills that were meant to knock her out, but she must have been taking them in the wrong order, because she fell asleep on the sofa all day, TV blaring, dribbling into the empty space at the top of the leg. She didn't put it away, anymore. It didn't leave her side. She even slept with it.

I moved in with a friend, Stacey, who taught me the important things – how to get free drinks in a bar by leaning forward and letting my tits spill out over my top; the perfect blowjob; never to speak first and not too much, and to always let a man think *he* came up with the answer. Stacey taught me it didn't matter what you did as long as you were thin and someone thought you pretty. She got me a job in the bar she worked at and things sometimes got a little out of hand. The tables speckled with white powder after a lock-in, sticky with ash and stale beer. Danny the cook with his wild eyes behind thick glasses, beads of sweat like diamonds. His swollen hands sharpening knives in the kitchen, wiping meat juices on his jeans, tripping up our skirts in the stock room. The regulars with their old, sad faces, watering eyes, wandering fingers. They said we reminded them of their daughters.

I went home rarely, if at all, and never at Christmas. At twenty, my mum brought out the leg for the final time and told me she'd been to the doctor, that she wasn't going to see me turn twenty-one, that the leg would be mine, now.

I took it home with me after the funeral to the small flat above the McDonald's on Bethnal Green Road that I shared with an Australian girl who changed lovers more often than she changed her sheets. I shut it away in a cupboard, along with my grief. It's still there, surrounded by boxes. I don't want it – I've never wanted it – but I can't quite bring myself to throw it away. It reminds me of home.

EARNEST MAGNITUDE'S INFINITE SADNESS

This is how it goes: I wake early, calm and serene, before I remember who and where I am and the dread gathers like a hungry cloud. I shake it off, literally; throw my legs – 'giraffe legs', Grandad used to call them, on account of them being so long and gangly and ungraceful, but I don't remember him calling any other parts of my body anything else because because he passed away a long time ago, a long time *see ya* but never *later alligator*, because there's no *later* when you're six feet under – over the edge of the bed.

My toes curl back from the cold wood floor, my knees pop the way they tend to do now I'm pushing fifty and my joints aren't what they used to be. People always seem surprised when I tell them I was an athlete at school; though it shouldn't be that shocking when you consider that giraffes are the tallest mammals on earth, with legs that are longer than most humans, and can run thirty-five miles per hour at a full sprint. And, okay, I may not run that much anymore, at forty-nine, and with a diet I admit is mostly convenience; though I do try to swallow bunches of kale when I can, because it's achingly hip, and if you smother it in oil and salt and fry it crispy it's not actually *that* bad, it tastes a little like the seaweed you get from a Chinese takeaway and slightly bitter, too; and if you choke it down then you're doing something good for your body and keeping up with the zeitgeist, all at the same time; but I *could* run, if I wanted to. And I should, probably; should probably do a little more to prevent my bottom from resembling one of those trucks that has a sign saying *Abnormal Load* at the back. Should probably go for a run in the woods near my house, but running now I'm forty-nine makes me feel like I'm dying, and I have enough thoughts of dying as it is to want to bring about my own personal hell by way of Nike trainers and Aztec yoga leggings.

Still, I stand and I wiggle my hips – *sizeable*, they are, *womanly*, even; though not *child-bearing*. No, no. Because there are too many children on the planet already, and that's not a comment on overpopulation as a whole, because in developed countries like Britain it's not the number of people that's really the problem but the way the capitalist machine blames poorer families who have more kids for all its social ills and evils, and makes it look like they're to blame, because there's no way they're going to allow anyone to dismantle our *ingrained plutocratic beliefs*; and that's what Deb says.

And I believe her, because instead of reading the trashy magazines that come in on subscription every month and get left on the big communal tables for everyone to pore over as a guilty pleasure, like I do, Deb always walks straight to non-fiction and picks out something clever about the climate crisis or economics and then tells me about it in digestible chunks while we're putting up displays of cut-out spiders and pumpkins in the kids' section for Halloween, or fluffy yellow chicks and cardboard eggs for Easter next to the automated machines you can use for 'returns' or 'renewals' without touching or talking to anyone, which is an important part of our world now, because of social distancing.

Deb says the establishment is pointing the political finger at families who have seven kids and live in a one-bedroom flat in a tower block on a run-down estate and is saying, it's *your* fault. But it's not the same in Britain as it is globally, it just isn't; it is *all* our faults, because we take a disproportionate toll on the planet, compared to children born in lower-income nations, even though we pretend that isn't the case and when we've finished with our own country we turn and point the political finger at Africa and Asia and Eastern Europe. But it is our fault, America's too; and I know that's true because I heard it on *Newsnight*.

And Deb, who wears the most wonderful headscarves, all intricate patterns, vibrant colours and soft curves wrapped around her head like ammonite, says that 'overpopulation' is the wrong word to use, and we should really be talking about 'overconsumption'; because the world population has increased sevenfold over the past two centuries which has stressed the planet out to its breaking point, Deb says, the planet is *stressed out*, and she makes a *stressed out* motion next to her head with her fingers. And I know what she means, she means that the planet is basically holding up its hands and saying, *guys – I can't take this anymore, I need some breathing room, okay?* And I know exactly how that feels because of Philip; because I too am suffocating in a sea filled with his files and folders and tea-stained papers on Ancient Greece, a pile that keeps getting larger even as his number of students gets smaller, every year; and when I tried to suggest that perhaps it's because the other lecturers *don't* clutter their houses with paper, that they're a more attractive proposition precisely *because* they take a more modern approach, using whiteboards or doing it all online, and Philip should really think about *moving with the times*, he just stared at me and I knew that in his head he was in Macedonia and not in Manor Park at all.

Look, I know it's hard, my love, I told him, because you're naturally old-fashioned, like one of those people who looks like they were born, already fifty, wearing a bow tie; and that's one of the reasons I love you, because you don't *care* about fashion or raves or cocktail bars or the latest thriller on Netflix, and I *adore* that about you but maybe we could make an appointment and go to Specsavers and try on some frameless glasses together, just once, what do you say? But he just looked at me again, blankly, so blankly, his shirt like one of his lecture notes, all spattered with coffee and untucked and his belly undulating softly like Hokusai's *Great Wave Off Kanagawa* and I could tell it was a losing battle; the way it's a losing battle every time I ask him to please *not* stuff handfuls of dry cereal into his mouth in the kitchen and crunch it right from the packet, standing up, gazing absently at the birds from the window; but to pour it into a bowl and eat it at the table. And I'm not sure I want to be with him anymore, and the crushing sadness that consumes me when I think about what *that* means is enough to send me beneath the duvet for hours, sometimes days. I'm like the planet; I just can't take it anymore. Not for *one* more second, though I'm delaying doing anything about it, because I'm so *used* to him, I really am; I really am far too stressed out to be single again, and it took me long enough to find Philip in the first place, and maybe it's okay to settle for a comfortable love, one that feels like you're pulling on a favourite jumper that's been washed a hundred times and is a bit bobbly but you're so accustomed to the way it fits that you don't even notice.

And Philip *never* notices. Not even when I'm wearing one of my brightest, most garish dresses, in colours that force the blues away. I have a rule that I wear a different, *vibrant* dress every single day, no matter how drab it is outside, how drab I feel inside, because wearing orange and gold can lift my spirits pretty much more than anything. I won't wear anything that doesn't bring me joy. Not one single item. What's the point in grey tracksuit bottoms and shapeless black sweater dresses that make you look and feel like a sack of potatoes, when you can wear a red and green peony-printed kimono wrap that looked good in the seventies, and okay, might be slightly *out there* for Tesco Express at 8am on a Tuesday, and turns heads, and not always in a kind way; but who cares when it makes some people smile, and helps you remember how to smile, too?

Thinking about the orange and gold dress conjures it up. I pull it from the rail of second-hand clothes that stands in the corner of my bedroom and leave it on top of the bed – let it bask there, triumphant at being chosen – while I go into the bathroom. I have another rule, a superficial one but it works: always wear lipstick. A bright red makes me *bold and alluring*, a soft pink makes me *girlish and coy*. A cool orange gives me *fire and fight*, right through to my fingertips, and a deep berry or plum, well, that's *power*. Anything can happen when I wear plum. Dorothy taught me never to go out of the house without something on my face; *make-up is like armour*, she said. She may have been bonkers, but she was always beautiful. Half of the dresses on my rail were hers; at least, the ones she didn't get rid of. She was always getting bored and throwing things away. Books, old letters, jewellery, husbands, me.

Today, I decide, is a plum day. And once I'm dressed in orange, gold and the requisite plum, I slip on my favourite pair of Birkenstocks, the ones so ancient and worn they feel like they've been carved into the soles of my feet, and head out without brushing my hair. I don't need to, not really, because these curls don't shift for anyone, and I enjoy feeling them bounce against my shoulders. My curls are always thrilled to be out. They love the promise in the early morning air, the scent of autumn roses.

I cross over at the lights, enter the forest on the south side. Head for the lake, as usual.

My lake, though not really; it just feels like mine because I love it so much, though I don't think anyone can really ever claim ownership over something so wild and wholly beautiful. I don't know the lake's name, don't want to know; but I do sometimes wonder if it's real or if it's a reflection of the kind of lake I always dreamed of living besides, the one I fancied I might one day wade into, my pockets filled with rocks, like Virginia Woolf. I still might.

I like to make a daily pilgrimage to the nameless lake, to sit for a moment on the little wooden bench covered in pigeon shit and chewing gum and teenage kisses. It is bright and clear, fresh without being cold, the dictionary definition of a September morning. The water is still, holding its breath. I can feel the smooth wood of the bench, hard and cool beneath my bottom; hear the distant whine of midges in the space around my right ear. Hear the satisfying *thwack* of someone hoofing a golf ball on the course nearby. I watch one of the swans take flight – wings like two enormous yachts sailed by billionaires through the ballpoint blue of the sky, orange beak *yaw yaw yawing* like a foghorn. It circles the penny outline of the water three times before slowing and landing, its cruisers come to rest. It drifts to the bank and nuzzles the reeds, overlooked by the heron sitting scornfully on top of a post in his grey overcoat, white bib untucked. I follow the swan's tracks through the wetlands towards, presumably, a nest; and let my eyes wander onwards, beyond the shallow beach and gritty mud slope that leads out of the water on the other side to a patch of dark grass, a clearing. And that's when I see him.

I squint. Shuffle forwards a bit to try and get a closer look, though it's a little pointless given he's right over there on the other side of the massive expanse, like a mirage, yet I still frown, and stand, and scan the outer reaches of the lake, and make the decision hastily, like I make most of my decisions: there's no question that I have to get there, get round to where he stands, take a closer look. I know it as bluntly and unequivocally as I know my own name: Earnest Magnitude, a towering fuck-up of a name, gifted to me by my mad mother, Dorothy Magnitude. Who knows if that was ever really our family name at all?

Not me, because I've never had one, never had a family full of kind old aunts who would bake flapjacks and invite us round for tea every weekend, and uncles who patted me awkwardly on the head and found shiny coins behind my ear. The kids at school boasted of Christmases with acres of cousins and grandparents who fell asleep snoring in pink velour and tipsy, giddy mums and dads who held hands like lovers as they gathered around a boxy screen to watch the Queen. Oceans of gravy and crisp, fluffy potatoes, drowning in goose fat. Mince pies served with brandy custard so thick you could use it as a pillow, striped stockings bursting with presents. Brothers, sisters. Babies. Not me. It was only ever just me and Dorothy. Plus Grandad, for a while, before he died. And he died over and over and over, at least in my head, because I loved him and the dead never stop dying, no matter how tired you are and how much you wish they wouldn't.

Dorothy said I was a miracle. Claimed she was a virgin when she conceived, christened me 'Earnest' in a fit of grandiosity, convinced I'd go on to become one of the greats – an opera singer, perhaps, or a television preacher. She loved those obscure American cable TV shows you found late at night on *The God Channel*, once you'd scrolled into the hundreds. She'd sit in her favourite, faded chair that she'd found on the street – "someone was just giving it away! Can you believe it, Earnest? Giving something like *this* –" she stroked the holes in the arms burnt through by cigarettes with one brightly-painted blue nail – "*away!*". Dorothy's obsessions waned and wavered as often as the moon, but nobody could have questioned her commitment to being pious. Towards the end, she used to give the other psych patients musical-inspired sermons, decked out in a bed-sheet like a barefoot Shirley Temple messiah.

Now, though. Now. I follow the path to the left rather than to the right, towards home. Push through leaves, almost lose my footing on a low-lying calamity of roots, all twisted together like they're fighting for air; reach out to steady myself against an old trunk covered in helter-skelter vines.

All the while, *he* dips in and out of my vision like he's playing peekaboo, watching me trip over myself, laughing at me trying to get there faster than my body will allow, like the time I had to race to hospital to see Grandad, and they told me I had hours, and I believed them, but after forty-five anxious minutes jiggling my knees on the Tube, and a hellish twenty-five minutes tapping my feet at the bus stop for the 55, then thirty stuck in traffic on the A201 through Elephant and Castle – at which point I was quite openly sobbing, and an old lady gave me a tissue from her bag that probably had lipstick or Covid-19 on it – I'd used them all up by the time I ran, using the giraffe legs Grandad used to tease me about, all the way to the entrance and up the wheelchair ramp and through the double doors with a buzzer on the outside; they'd turned the machines off that were helping him breathe, and he was gone. I was too late.

An empty web strung delicately between two branches brushes my face and I claw at my skin like it's trying to eat me. There's nothing I dislike more than spiders, except racists. I once played a game of 'would you rather' with Deb and honestly couldn't decide whether I'd rather have dinner with a spider or with a Tory. Not that all Tories are racists, of course, except that they mostly are. Like that awful woman who looks after her grandson and who brought him in for *Rhyme Time* last Thursday, when little Jamal was in too, with *his* grandma, and Jamal is the sweetest, kindest little boy with the biggest smile, and he knows all the words to *I'm A Little Teapot* and does it *with* the actions, he's achingly bright; there aren't many other two-year-olds who enunciate the word 'stout' the way *he* enunciates 'stout', with such a perfect, sibilant 's', but the awful woman, who's quite obviously a Tory, took an instant dislike to Jamal and three guesses why *that* was.

And she started stirring it up; started stage whispering to her grandson – making a point about something by talking *through* him, her little curly-haired blonde grandson, who's perfectly well-behaved himself and it's not his fault he has a racist grandma, it's just a shame that she has any influence at all over his future views. And she was whispering pointedly to him about how there were 'troublemakers' there today; only because she had to disguise her vitriol, she said "troublywubbly makers", which got her a few disgusted looks as it is. And she kept on and on about how they shouldn't let *just anyone* in, and how they should make people pay in advance, and sign up online, so they could cap the numbers — the "numbee-wumbees" she said, honest to God — before things went "too far".

Too far, like what, exactly? I wanted to ask and was about to, I was rolling up my metaphorical sleeves and putting down the literal pile of DVDs we still stock even though nobody watches DVDs anymore, because nobody has a DVD player anymore; though I had been rather enjoying putting them away while listening to Deb trilling all the songs for *Rhyme Time*. I'd planned to high-five her afterwards, about her swapping round the words to *The Wheels On The Bus*, because we always ranted about how diminishing it was to have the daddies on the bus saying, "Stop that noise! Stop that noise!" while the mummies on the bus just go, "chatter chatter chatter", as though that's all women do, chatter incoherently, about irrelevant topics, while men tell us to be quiet — though that does happen, of course, and that's why we need to keep the feminist fight alive at all times, because it starts early, it really does, and never earlier than with nursery rhymes. And then *this* happened.

I turned my head to see this vile woman staring at little Jamal like she was chewing on a wasp, and Jamal's grandma didn't say anything because *she's* well-mannered, she didn't even meet her eye, just stared regally ahead, and I wanted to bend my knee and kiss her queenly hand right there. I shifted my gaze and glared at Deb, giving her the jabbing side-eye look we've cultivated to clue each other in when someone's being an arse — but Deb had clocked it already, of course, and piped up with, "Yes, we *have* been having a problem with numbers, you're quite right, and we are over-subscribed today, I had hardly noticed but now I have, I can't possibly continue, but how *kind* of you to offer to leave now so that we can continue to socially-distance in the safest way for everybody." I gave Deb an extra powerful high-five, after that.

And I'm so busy thinking about Jamal that I don't notice the two beeches trapped in an endless, erotic embrace, and I don't see the mess of roots bursting from the ground to face the sky like a curled lip after an argument; and I don't feel the ground rushing up towards my face like a firework until I'm face-down, tasting soil.

I sigh into the damp earth. What am I doing? Chasing after a dream – the dream I saw from the other side of the lake, and I'm worn out, because it's bigger than I realised, the lake; I don't think I've ever actually walked all the way around it, not once since I moved here, even though it's been ten years. Ten years since I finally left our tiny flat in Bethnal Green, with the lift that'd been broken since the dark ages, and the wonky shopping trolley marooned at the bottom of the stairwell like a Tracey Emin installation. The stairwell bathed in the ethereal light of a flickering bulb, barely breaking the perpetual gloom. The *rush rushing* sound of the fire-safe door as it opened, black fringe at the bottom sticking like cement on the tangled mess of takeaway leaflets, bills and adverts for dry cleaning. The clink of the chain to shut the world out, to sink into the tears, dents and stray bits of foam of Dorothy's favourite chair, long grown cold in the corner.

The scent of canned saltwater fish, cranked open and fried with rice, onions and a dash of balsamic vinegar to make 'Tuna Surprise', one of Dorothy's favourites, her *signature dish* that she taught me to make after a trip to the 24 hour Tesco at one or two in the morning, because she liked to do her shopping long after everyone else was in bed, unhindered by screaming children, shouting mothers and dangerously dawdling pensioners, and she got the best bargains then, too, and said it didn't matter if I was tired the next day at school because I was learning *vital life lessons*. And she'd rattle up 'Tuna Surprise', or tell me to, when we got back, even though it was almost dawn and I had a maths test at nine. She'd eat it from her chair, next to the fire, in front of Audrey Hepburn, and I'd curl up on the dirty pink sofa that scratched my legs and fight to stay awake. Then she'd shuffle to bed and sleep until noon, and I'd have to force myself out of bed at half seven and pull on my school uniform, though I could barely see because I was so tired, and I'd usually forget to brush my hair and my teeth and that's why kids at school started calling me *Eurgh*-nest, and they'd hold their noses as they said it, and wave their hands around, and said I smelled rotten, which to be fair I probably did, but it still hurt.

And now I smell of mud and the faint whiff of fox shit lingering on a snarl of leaves nearby. I sigh again and press the palms of my hands against the forest floor to heave myself up. The horizon slips, because I haven't had breakfast, yet; but looking back at the bench over on the other side of the lake steadies me, and also tells me he should be *just* ahead. That's where the clearing is. I've made it. So why am I so nervous?

My mouth is dry, and I'm doing that thing I do whenever I have to speak in public, which is swallow constantly because it feels like if I don't, my throat is in danger of closing up on me and leaving me no room to breathe, no room at all. Like the time I had to chair a reading with that terribly handsome

132

'weird' fiction writer, who came all the way to the local community hall attached to the side of our little library, and arrived all tattooed and single-earringed and shaved-headed and smelling of rain and salt and windswept cliffs in Cornwall where you go walking in the middle of a storm, and your hair is whipped into a spike and your cheeks burn and you're grinning, you can't stop grinning, because despite the awful weather you've never felt more *alive*. And I had to sit on stage next to this glorious man, whose words I adore, and feel the weight of his Heathcliff gaze on my face as I stared back at him, transfixed, and threw a breathless rush of questions at him, and intermittently swallowed and swallowed, simply to stay alive.

The best thing to do when you're anxious about something is to get it over with. That's what Grandad used to say when I'd cling on to his leg, begging him not to make me go to school, because I couldn't take the taunts and jeers a moment longer, and I didn't like having to line up for free school dinners, while the other kids ate packed lunches their mums and dads had lovingly made for them, with tiny boxes of raisins and sandwiches cut into perfect triangles, which my mum didn't do. And I didn't like the way they spat in my direction and shouted things about Dorothy *in the loony bin* and laughed in a mean way and stuck balls of chewing gum in my hair which was impossible to get out without hacking at it with the kitchen scissors, tears streaming down my face. *Just get it over with*, Grandad would say in the mornings, when he was looking after me because she *was*, Dorothy *was* in the loony bin, but it was just because she was so sensitive, that's what Grandad said, and he said I was the same but I had something extra going for me, because I had *resilience*. And he'd give me a firm and no-nonsense push in the direction of the school gate, and I'd keep my face set like a Japanese noh mask, purposefully neutral, because it's difficult to tell the actual feelings expressed in a noh mask, even though the mask carver tries to instil a variety of emotions; and I didn't want anybody to see me crying.

Get it over with. I repeat it now like a mantra, as I crunch over curious leaves towards the clearing. I feel like I'm about to stumble on something big, that it is going to mean something important, and I wonder if it'll be one of those moments I'll write down in my journal when I get home, and then years later will look back and read about it and reflect that it was the point that *everything changed*; and I hope for that, I hope it's *that* outcome, and not one that wears the crushing scent of disappointment.

Brambles snatch at my clothes like cats. My chin throbs, bears the kiss of the earth. What was I doing, falling over, like that? Just toppling right out of my grave, unsteady? Philip will tut in that way he does when I tell him what happened. He'll fetch the witch hazel and soak a piece of cotton wool and dab at me haphazardly, but gently, leaving me smelling of herbs and wet newspaper and quiet, steady love. And my mind is still on Philip, on the solidity of him – because Philip has never been shadow, he's never lacked outline and needed to be drawn in, he leaves boot prints from his size 10 too-yellow Timberlands in mud and concrete and on the floorboards in our tiny Victorian mid-terrace, because Philip doesn't notice mess even when he is the architect of it – when I break out into the clearing. And I'm dazzled, suddenly, by the openness of it; my eyes awash with a light so bright, so shimmering and radiant and *green*, so green that it fills my nostrils and the lenses of my eyes pick out only green; a green so verdant that I smell hidden pine forests leaning dangerously from the side of a mountain, see piles of jewelled ornaments in an enchanted palace and hear Dorothy – not my mother, *the* Dorothy – tip-toeing carefully around, trying to pick the right green treasure to save her friends from the Nome King and Mombi and her endless, screaming heads. It is an algae-like green clinging to the bottom of a boat drifting in the shallows of a Cornish fishing village, the fizzing salt-scent of kelp laid out on shore like a sacrifice; the green of freshly-cut grass, fingers stained wet; a stiff green, tinged with white, because of Sports' Day, and you get called up to leap over hurdles because you're tall, because everyone thinks that makes you graceful. It is a wet, slick, lichen green, the green of a bed of soft moss that you could lie down on to make love, to yourself or to someone deserving; a dark, sultry green, a forest green, green. The rich browns and greens of a majestic oak, two hundred years old or more. Roots spread thick as army boots, muscled arms open and wide. He stands, entirely occupying the space around him, like Thor commanding the heavens. I stand before him, a disciple, transfixed. In his gaze I am exulted. More than that: I am *aroused*. I've never seen anything more beautiful. And I think of Ali Smith, of that story she wrote, *May*, about a woman who falls in love with the whiteness of blossom adorning the branches of a tree in her neighbour's garden so beautiful it could make your mouth water, and I suddenly understand exactly where she was coming from when she wrote the words, "I tell you. I fell in love with a tree. I couldn't not."

I don't know how long I stand before him, eyes ravenously eating every inch, but it's long enough that the freshness of September seeps into my bones, chilling me from the inside out, and my hips throb from standing, and I stretch out my hand like I'm trailing my fingers in cold water to graze the surface of his skin. He is electric. He leaves me unsteady.

And then it is dark, too soon, and I have to go home, and somehow the whole day has passed and *oh, God*, I am wretched! I don't *want* to go back to my life! I can feel him inside me, racing through my capillaries like poison, like Romeo's vial, taken too soon; and it feels like I'm wearing gloves with electrodes inside them – two giant, skin-covered gloves – and I can't move properly because they're full to bursting, and I'm scared.

Because I don't know what it means to want something this much and to not be able to have it. It's like fire-ants, beneath my skin; like Orwell's *1984*, and I'm inside my very own personal hell, inside Room 101, and beneath the box I can't move away from is the obliterating absence of touch. And I don't know if it's the fact that I've not been touched in so long, because Philip stopped touching me years ago, said we were *too old for that nonsense*, and that's why we have separate bedrooms, though occasionally he comes in and hovers at my doorway in a pair of clean pyjamas, fresh and shiny pink from the bath, and I know that he's hovering with *intent*, but the very idea of touching him, of being touched by him, both simultaneously appals and overwhelms me. It's different to the way I suddenly, violently need to feel the scratch of rough bark.

I want my soft openings to be probed with wood, my insides scraped a soft, mossy green. I want to plunge twigs and branches and budding shoots inside myself again and again, over and over; I'll do anything, beg to be allowed to do anything if I can only consume him and be consumed. I want to eat and be eaten, devoured and destroyed and hurt and left bruised and aching, shuddering and spent. To be soiled. To walk home limping, skin torn and scratched; wear him drenched across my body, take him wet and green and slippery in my mouth, push him deep into my throat until I gag.

And what if I never get over this feeling? This feeling of being completely and utterly invisibly alone, even in a crowded room full of people, like I'm living inside a bubble nobody else can see? I could reach out and touch the thin skin of the world with my finger, could scrape the inner shell until it threatens to tear, until it wrinkles and dries up, leaving me breathless, but how can I breathe without love? How can *anyone* breathe without love?

I thought I didn't need it, thought I would never, fully feel it, because I lived for years with love as a dress rehearsal, waiting for the main event; always felt like an understudy for love, struggling to memorise my lines, petrified of being called to the stage, of being thrust into the spotlight and found lacking, of not receiving bunches of red roses at the end of the show but a review in the local news that only gave me one star; tried so hard to confine love to a dozen scratches in the bedpost, to the width of a mattress, a feather-down semblance of love, light of tog, love as a lightweight sheet you want to pull to your chin in winter and kick off in summer because it's hot and weighty and suffocating.

I take a few steps towards home before turning back, letting my hand trail to my side. What if he's not there when I come back? Should I stay? If I am to stay, I'll need a coat. Something to drink. Maybe something to sit on. And the hope of that – for it is a warm, soft hope, a promise, really, for there was never any question that I wouldn't come back, it was written, but by whom I couldn't say, and all I know is that it is the certainty of my return that finally lets me leave.

I wake the next morning to pale light streaming in through the floral curtains, the type of sunshine which, when it's refracted through rain-splattered windows, always seems meek and timid, weaker than it should; and it's a shame because I like to feel strong in the mornings, if I can, if it's a good day and I manage to shake off all the dread. Only this morning, the dread doesn't come. Where darkness would usually begin to gather like a funeral procession, I can only think of him. Magnificent. Erotic. Green.

I slide my hand beneath the heat of the covers, my hand warm against my belly's dimpled softness. Close my eyes and conjure up seventeen sturdy branches, thick enough to be trees in their own right, shooting skywards. Stiff, proud, dripping with sap. Trace a line with one finger slowly down from my bellybutton, and my body reacts – it's been so long since I was touched! – my ribcage stiffens, I hear my own sharp intake of breath like I'm outside my body, looking in; goosebumps spring up like water. My breasts are firm and soft at the same time, my nipples pink and puckered, and stroking them sends delicious jolts of electricity to my groin, like serpents, like flickers of poison from forked tongues, like Medusa. Behind my eyelids, the steady thrust and pulse of emerald, until the ceiling trembles like a canopy.

I lie still, catching my breath, breathless and wondering. What outrageous fortune is this? To be basking in the first flush of desire, to feel like a girl, again? The cliches are true, which is why they are cliches, I suppose, and I'll admit it: I've never felt so alive. It's like I've been born again. Life, suddenly, has a purpose. *He* is my purpose. It feels so obvious, all of a sudden, like all of the saccharine song lyrics were really onto something. And I'm in the middle of my morning routine, more energised than ever, legs thrown over the side of the bed, as usual – though nothing feels usual, not now, not anymore – when something wild happens in the kitchen. I freeze, my heart bobbing like a fishing rod. *Philip.*

I throw my bedroom door open, pausing for half a second to appreciate how *dramatic* this scene is; I'm like a woman running after a train as it pulls away from the station in the 1940s, her lover on board, and she's desperate and disconsolate, all at once, because on some level she believes that if he doesn't look back out of the train window to see her there, if he doesn't look back, then he'll never come back, and their great love will be lost; though mine isn't lost, it *isn't*, it's been *found*, for the first time – and then I hear Philip howl like he's cut some of himself clean off, and I rush downstairs, taking them three at a time, and discover that's exactly what he's done.

And I feel bad but I'm also frustrated with him. *Philip,* I say, *I've got important things to do today, couldn't you have been more careful?* I tut, quite audibly, I can't help myself, and I wrap a piece of kitchen roll around his finger. *What a thrill,* I tell him, trying to lighten the mood, *my thumb instead of an onion.* And he looks at me with his brows all crumpled like an accordion, and asks me what I'm talking about, and he sounds quite cross as he remarks sharply that it's not his thumb it's his 'pinky', and that's what he calls it, and it makes me laugh, because to hear a Professor of Ancient Greek History use the word 'pinky' is funny, somehow. No, silly, I tell him. It's Sylvia Plath. *"The top quite gone, except for a sort of hinge of skin, a flap like a hat, dead white. Then that red plush."* I know *Cut*, by heart, like I know most of Sylvia's work by heart. And that's what it looks like, Philip, I explain. Your finger. The top quite gone, except for this dead flap, and that red plush, all soaking through the kitchen roll. And I show him his blood, seeping like a rose across the patterned paper. But then Philip starts to go all grey and glassy, and he moans a little, and then he says he thinks he might need to sit down.

I hook one of the kitchen chairs around my ankle and drag it over, help him sit down, and I crouch before him and make sympathetic *shhhing* noises, but I'm fretting, I admit it; that's the only word for it, because Marjorie will be awful if I'm late for work, she really will, she's been banging on for months about how at risk we are, because of the *economic devastation wrought by Rona*, that's what Marjorie likes to call it, *Rona*, like the virus is a member of the W.I, knitting blankets, accidentally dropping a stitch; and Marjorie says hundreds of libraries could be closed forever, not to mention the decade of austerity *in which 773 such centres were already shut down, folks, that's the level of risk we're facing, here,* and she nods almost smugly, it feels like, like a part of her is almost glad so many have shut down so she can really hammer home how precious ours is, or was; and I hate the way she refers to libraries as *centres*, I really do, it just doesn't feel right, though I suppose that's not the point, it's not at all the point; but anyway such closures may *pale* alongside the fallout from *Rona*, that's what Marjorie says, and it sounds bloody terrible, don't get me wrong, but it also sounds particularly bloody terrible thanks to the way she says it.

But mostly I'm annoyed because I'd figured that I could afford to leave 20 minutes early to get to the forest to see him, to get my fix, because feasting on beauty is the best nourishment there is, and it's quite impossible to keep away from someone when you're in the first flushes of romance. And yet: here I am, holding a blood-soaked piece of kitchen roll that looks like it's been used to mop up after a crime scene, like there should be police tape cordoning Philip off; and my knees are hurting so I have to stand up, but as soon as I come out of my crouch I spot the top end of his pinky on the work-top and I pick it up gingerly and stare at it, because I've never held a piece of someone before, a body part, or anything, when it's not been attached to the rest of them.

I don't know what to do with it except drop it in a glass of milk, and I feel sort of woozy myself, to be honest; it's kind of disgusting, but I'm also transfixed by the sight of this small chunk of him bobbing around in the glass of milk, and so I don't really listen to Philip, but when I tune in I realise he's saying something about teeth, and he is, he *is* talking about teeth, and what he's saying is *it's lost teeth you put in milk, Earnest, not soft tissue*, and I think I've accidentally dissolved Philip's pinky.

But I can't find it within myself to be shattered by this terrible wrongness, I just can't, because all the while my mind keeps flicking back to green. Mr Green, I think I'll call him, on account of not knowing his name yet, but I don't know if he'd be the type to use an honorific; it seems too stiff and too formal, when he's the *opposite* of that: he is wild and free and elemental, wind and sky and the shock rush of the rain. And I know I sound irritated with Philip, but I can't help it, he's made me lose my train of thought, which was full of chlorophyll; my mind is creeping, budding ivy, I can't concentrate when to do so would mean pruning myself back with twine. *You seem distracted, Earnest, is anything the matter?* Philip is saying, and by the tone of his voice I can tell it's the second or third time he's said it, I just haven't answered yet; and I am immediately on guard. *What do you mean*, I spit out, like I'm part of a firing squad, all shooting at once to allay any individual guilt; *what do you mean, I'm not distracted, why would I be distracted?*

Philip is staring at me with that look he gets when he can't work something out, the one he gets when he does sudoku in the paper, or when we used to go to pub quizzes and try to answer questions about pop music, because if it's not classical then Philip won't know about it, Ariana Grande could give him a private concert and Philip would smile absently and tap his foot, completely out of time, and struggle to make eye contact, and wonder who on earth the young, talented, beautiful woman in front of him was, and why she was wasting her time performing for him. Because Philip has never, ever felt deserving, thanks to his mother, the vicar's wife; who had a penchant for *penance* and *damnation*, and passed on that expectation on to her poor, sweet son. And I know Philip's feeling anxious; I can't see his tongue but I know he's running it against the back of his lower teeth; can picture its redness flicking side-to-side like a grass snake, the way he does when he feels unsure of himself and doesn't know what to do about it. And I'm sorry for that, I really am, but it's true that I have a secret. It's true. I am alight.

Once the drama of the lost pinky subsides, Philip's wound starts to heal; but we are fractured. I find myself spending less and less time at home *or* at work, and I even start avoiding Deb, because she thinks something is wrong, when it couldn't be more right, and I can't believe she can't see that, yet she keeps leaving books open from the self-help section, pointing to words like *dissociation* and *delayed trauma* and *getting help*.

And then I get arrested, but I don't want to talk about that.

Then after I get let out, and they close the forest on account of what happened, and I've got campaigners at my door as well as the press, I hole up at home and Philip catches me climbing out through the window in the middle of the night and calls the police because we're two floors up, and if they can't stop me, nobody will. And Philip, who usually frowns in a patient sort of a way, finally snaps; he bunches his hands into small fists, and puffs himself up, bless him, standing as tall and as mightily as he can for all five feet six inches of him, and he blows out his chest, and squares his shoulders, and he has these bright red triangles on both cheeks. And he takes one look at the devastation of my face and says, *where is he, Earnest*; *where is this cad who's broken your heart*, and he really does use the word *cad*, and that's so divinely Philip, and then his eyes look wildly left and right, and his face splits in two, and half of it slides down and plops wetly to the floor and I realise that's because I'm crying, all of a sudden; great, desperate sobs that swell up from somewhere deep inside me, like a hosepipe has suddenly been turned on after a summer drought, with the flowers and the grass simultaneously sighing and gasping in unison from the shock of it.

I can't stop the terrible swell, though there's snot running from both nostrils down my face and I know I must look *awful*, just *hideous*, really; but I can't stop, no matter how many times I sniff, because my nose has gone all stuffy, even though it's running at the same time, and I can't seem to breathe in any air at all. And I know, because I remember it from school, that it's because of the *nasolacrimal ducts*, the *nasolacrimal ducts* that run down each side of the nose, and the tears flow into them and mix with the nasal mucus. And when we cry, even more tears travel down through the *nasolacrimal ducts* into our noses, which get all stuffy and we sniff to try and get the tears out of there, but when we do that we actually pull them further into our throats and we swallow them: we swallow all our tears.

And I'm so busy swallowing all my tears that I barely notice Philip leading me softly to bed, and when he reappears and stands awkwardly in the doorway, holding a hot mug of tea for me, all I can do is stare at him and nod, gasping and sniffing and gulping, while he waits, not knowing if it's alright for him to come in, if I want him there; but I *do* want him there, I do, and he asks if I would like some tea and I smile through all the snot and the swallowed tears and I say *yes please, Philip.* Yes, please.

ACKNOWLEDGMENTS

Sylvia Plath watches us sleep, but we don't mind won third prize in The London Magazine's short story competition, 2018.

Drowning doesn't look like drowning was longlisted in the Commonwealth Short Story Competition 2019 – the source on drowning was taken from <u>On Scene Magazine: Fall 2006</u> (page 14, Francesco A. Pia).

The girl in the photograph was longlisted in The Guardian's The Bazaar of Bad Dreams Writing Competition, judged by Stephen King.

Tsuris was a runner up in the Unbound Short Story Competition, 2016.

The boat was first published by Spread the Word's Flight Journal, Issue 5.

Below the line was first published in the The Word for Freedom anthology: short stories for women's suffrage, in 2018.

About Fly on the Wall Press

A publisher with a conscience.
Political, Sustainable, Ethical.
Publishing politically-engaged, international fiction, poetry and cross-genre anthologies on pressing issues. Founded in 2018 by founding editor, Isabelle Kenyon.

Some other publications:

The Sound of the Earth Singing to Herself by Ricky Ray

We Saw It All Happen by Julian Bishop

Odd as F*ck by Anne Walsh Donnelly

Imperfect Beginnings by Viv Fogel

These Mothers of Gods by Rachel Bower

Sin Is Due To Open In A Room Above Kitty's by Morag Anderson

Fauna by David Hartley

How To Bring Him Back by Clare HM

Hassan's Zoo and A Village in Winter by Ruth Brandt

No One Has Any Intention of Building A Wall by Ruth Brandt

Snapshots of the Apocalypse by Katy Wimhurst

Demos Rising

Exposition Ladies by Helen Bowie

A Dedication to Drowning by Maeve McKenna

The House with Two Letterboxes by Janet H Swinney

Climacteric by Jo Bratten

Cracked Asphalt by Sree Sen

The State of Us by Charlie Hill

Social Media:

@fly_press (Twitter) @flyonthewallpress (Instagram)

@flyonthewallpress (Facebook)

www.flyonthewallpress.co.uk